# BOUND IN CRIMSON

*Blood Oath #1*

J.A. CARTER

*Bound in Crimson*

Published by J.A. Carter

Copyright © 2021 by J.A. Carter

www.authorjacarter.com

Cover Design: Keylin Rivers

All rights reserved. Without limiting the rights under copyright reserved above, no part of this publication may be reproduced, stored in or introduced into retrieval system, or transmitted, in any form, or by any means (electronic, mechanical, photocopying, recording, or otherwise) without the prior written permission of both the copyright owner and the above publisher of this book.

This is a work of fiction. Names, characters, places, brands, media, and incidents are either the products of the author's imagination or are used fictitiously. The author acknowledges the trademarked status and trademark owners of various products referenced in this work of fiction, which have been used without permission. The publication/use of these trademarks is not authorized, associated with, or sponsored by the trademark owners.

## ALSO BY J.A. CARTER

*Blood Oath* Series
*Bound in Crimson*
*Tempted by Fire*
*Entangled in Scarlet*
*Fated in Ruby*
*Unraveled by Desire*

AUTHORS NEED REVIEWS!

Once you've read *Bound in Crimson*, please consider leaving a review on Amazon and Goodreads. Reviews are so important for authors to find new readers!

## BLURB

**I should hate them, yet there's no denying my body reacts to their every touch.**

When my ancestors lost everything in a business deal gone wrong, they were forced to make a sacrifice—a blood oath, promising the firstborn daughter of their bloodline to a league of vampires.

And now they've come to collect.

Atlas.
Kade.
Gabriel.
Lex.
All seductively sexy and unimaginably dangerous.

Torn from everything I've ever known, they take me captive in their Washington, D.C. mansion.

Each is determined to own me—body, heart, and soul. I'd be lying if I said the thought of that didn't make my skin tingle in anticipation. Still, the alluring immortals are in for a surprise, because ancient debt aside, I'm not going down without a fight.

*This one's for me.*

## I

There are four vampires in my living room.

The space is blanketed in darkness save for the dim light cast against the aged hardwood floor from the one window in the room. It's closed—painted shut by the previous tenant—but the chirp of a car horn in the distance still rings through the silence.

None of them move. One leans against the exposed brick wall near my flat-screen, while the others occupy the light gray L-shaped couch I saved up for months to afford.

*Do they think I can't see them?* Surely they can hear the thundering heartbeats in my chest.

I stand frozen in the entryway, my key still in the lock. My eyes shift to the clock on the stove in my kitchen. It's almost one in the morning. Tonight has already been long, full of studying at the campus library, but the pit in my stomach tells me it's about to get a lot fucking worse.

My right leg shifts back.

"Don't run."

That smooth, deep, siren-like voice tries to trick my brain into keeping my feet anchored in place, but I know better. I whirl around, dropping my book bag in the doorway as I bolt for the bank of elevators at the end of the hall.

My heart slams against my chest in time with my white Doc Martens hitting the polished floor with each stride.

"Calla."

I swallow a yelp, turning to look over my shoulder as I keep running, only to find the hallway empty.

I slide to a halt and slam my fist against the elevator button, throwing myself inside the second it slides open. It's only once the door has shut that I let out a shaky breath. I inhale slowly, fighting the urge to scream until my throat is raw.

*This can't be happening. Not yet.*

Pressing the button for the lobby, I fall back against the wall, my eyes burning with exhaustion. Panic floods in when I realize what a terribly stupid move that was. They'll head straight for the lobby. I chew my lip for a second and press the button to the sixth floor. The elevator descends as the numbers count down *10, 9, 8, 7, 6* and it slows to a stop. The soft *ding* makes me push off the wall and step out into the quiet hallway.

I have no idea what the hell I'm doing. All I know is that I can't go back to the fifteenth floor and I can't go to the lobby. I'm trapped.

Unless…

They likely took the stairs down to the lobby and are waiting for the elevator—and my dumb ass.

I walk toward the door to the stairwell. I can take that down to the parking garage and slip out onto the street from there.

The door slams shut behind me, echoing off the concrete walls and stairs. I grip the cold metal railing as I race down the flights, noting the floor number painted in bright yellow on the wall at each landing.

My deep brown hair clings to the back of my neck. I suck in a shallow breath as my feet hit the landing on the second floor and the door to the hallway flies open.

I don't have time to scream. In the time it takes me to blink, I'm against the wall. Hands grip my shoulders, pressing my back into the concrete. My dull brown gaze flies up and collides with swirling silver irises.

I immediately turn feral. I fight against his grip, kicking and scratching at his chest with my chipped emerald fingernails. It doesn't faze him. And when I open my mouth to scream, he quickly clamps his hand over it before I can make a sound.

He exhales slowly. "Atlas told you not to run." His voice is low, tinged with amusement. He's enjoying this.

It takes every ounce of strength I have to rip his hand away from my mouth. He returns that hand to my shoulder, tightening his hold on me.

"I don't give a shit. Let go of me," I say through my teeth, trying to escape his grip as my heavy breathing makes the world spin around me.

He cocks his head, and his dark brown hair falls into his face. "If I do that, you'll run again." The twitch of his lips has me thinking that's exactly what he wants. *They love the chase.*

"I'll scream," I warn, shoving against him again. I'm no match for his strength, though knowing that doesn't convince me to stop. If anything, it makes me fight harder. It's what has kept me motivated every single morning to wake at the crack of dawn and spend at least an hour at the gym. Training regularly to build my strength for this exact moment. I've managed a bit of muscle on my sadly curve-free figure but compared to these guys, I'm tiny. I was kidding myself that I'd stand a chance against a vampire—let alone four. Years of training, and it was all for nothing. My stomach plummets at the thought; I'm not ready to admit it.

"You will," he agrees, "though it'll be my name before it's anything else." The vampire in front of me pushes me back, lowering his face to mine. "But by all means, give it a shot." He knows as well as I do it won't get me anywhere.

"Who the fuck are you?" I growl instead, ignoring the way his words made my heart race. It's a dumb question, but if I can keep him talking maybe I can buy myself some time to figure a way out of this mess.

The guy smirks, a subtle twist of his lips that would make the purest of angels desire sin. "You know who I am. You ran because you know exactly who we are."

I grit my teeth when his fingers flex against my bare shoulders. It doesn't hurt, but his proximity is making my knees shake. Though that could also be from sprinting down the stairs. "I ran because it's the middle of the night and you broke into my apartment."

Those silver eyes snare me without effort and sparkle. "Calla, Calla, Calla."

I scowl when he tuts his tongue, and swallow the bile rising in my throat. "Stop saying my name."

He grins. "Are you going to play nice if I step away now?"

"That depends," I say, "if you consider me punching you in the face playing nice."

He whistles softly. "You're going to be quite the handful, aren't you?"

That catches my attention, and I stiffen.

"Kade, that's enough." The voice comes from above, and my head turns in time to see another silver-eyed guy walking down the concrete stairs toward us. This one isn't as muscular as the guy holding me against the wall—Kade apparently—and he has wavy copper hair with strands that appear pure gold in this light. It's a mess of waves that I can't stop staring at.

"Relax, Gabriel. She's fine. Aren't you, Calla?" He hooks

my chin with his finger and turns my gaze back to him. The moment our eyes meet, a pleasant warmth floods through me, washing away the tension in my muscles.

I nod without a single thought. Of course, I'm fine. I can't even remember what I could have possibly been upset about.

Kade smiles, and I find myself smiling back… until he blinks, severing the glamour.

I stare at him for several seconds, horrified by my complete loss of control, and then I lose my shit. Tension grips me again as my eyes narrow, and I curl my fingers against my palms. "You fucking pr—"

Gabriel pulls me away from him before I can start throwing fists. "All right, angel, let's go."

In the brief moment he lets go of my arm, I duck under his and run. My grip on the railing slips from the dampness of my palm, but I manage to grab it again before falling. I make it to the next landing and collide with Gabriel's chest.

My head whips back toward the level above where he'd just been, and I shake my head as I struggle to catch my breath.

"Stop running," he says in a voice so soft, so gentle, I pause. He isn't glamouring me.

I take a step away, and I'm about to tell him where he can go when my back hits a solid wall of muscle. I turn to find Kade grinning at me, and my eyes burn with angry tears.

*There's no way out.*

"Calla." Gabriel's smooth voice makes me look back at him.

I shake my head, cursing myself as one awful word leaks from my lips. "Please."

"Oh, come on," Kade says, wrapping his arm around my shoulders and holding me against his side. "Don't start begging now. I much prefer your sharp tongue."

My brows knit as anger crackles through me once more,

and I grit my teeth. "Fuck you," I seethe, shoving away from him.

Gabriel steps in, placing his hand at the small of my back, guiding me toward the hallway. The warmth of his hand surprises me, though I'm not sure why, and all of a sudden, it doesn't matter. We're moving out of the stairwell, back into the hallway to the elevator bank.

"See? That's much better," Kade says from behind us, and I inhale slowly to keep myself from launching at him again. Theoretically, I know it won't get me anywhere, but that sure as hell doesn't mean I'm restrained enough to ignore the urge.

We get into the elevator, and Gabriel presses the button to my floor as the door slides shut, then he leans against the wood-paneled wall. He rakes his fingers through those copper curls, and my eyes roam over him, taking in his formal appearance. Dark slacks and a starch white collared shirt make him look as if he came here from some sort of business meeting. Especially compared to the distressed jeans and the T-shirt that is barely containing Kade's insane muscles. Gabriel looks to be a few years older than him, though both have at least a century on me. Despite that—and the reason they're here—I can't help but notice how attractive they are. Would I prefer to not have them in my life? Of course. Perhaps if we'd met in a bar instead of my apartment in the middle of the night, I might've let them buy me a drink. But that isn't our circumstance.

I'd like to think I can chalk up my physical attraction toward them to their vampiric allure. All humans are drawn to it despite—for the majority of the population—being oblivious to the existence of vampires, so how could I possibly think I'd be immune?

I stare at the stubble along Kade's defined jaw, watching as a muscle feathers along it. Despite his outward amusement to the situation, he's tense too. And if that doesn't put me on edge even more... *What the hell does he have to be worried about?*

Kade hums under his breath—a Pink Floyd song, I think —as the elevator ascends, and my jaw is clenched so hard my molars are throbbing by the time we step off on the fifteenth floor. When we reach my apartment, Kade opens the door and walks in as if he owns the place. I follow him inside with Gabriel behind me and faintly notice my book bag is hung on the hook next to my jacket. Someone has turned on the light above my kitchen island as well as the few lamps around my living room, blanketing the relatively small space in warm light.

The other two guys are still sitting on my couch. Waiting. They knew Kade and Gabriel would have no issues returning with me, and I hate that.

Kade walks over and drops onto the end of the couch. It's unsettling how comfortable he seems in my apartment. Like maybe this isn't his first time here... A chill runs through me, and I push the thought away. I can't think about that now.

"Calla Montgomery," a new voice says, and another of the guys gets off the couch and walks toward me.

My breath halts as I take him in. He's dressed in black from head to toe in wrinkle-free pants and a button-up shirt that makes him look as if he's about to attend a charity banquet. His hair is a deep brown, cropped on the sides and slightly longer on top, but styled expertly, not a piece out of place. His face is all sharp angles, paired with dark brows and thick lashes. He's tall and built like Kade, and definitely not the kind of person you'd want to meet in a dark alley—or anywhere for that matter. My body tenses, recognizing the vampire before me as a predator. Everything about him warns me away and pulls me closer in the same breath. It's a contradiction that makes my head spin. He's different than the others. I don't know why or what it is about him that makes me realize it, but there's something about him... I reel my thoughts in. Now is *not* the time to debate this.

I press my lips together for a moment. "If I say you have the wrong person, will you leave?"

Kade chuckles from the couch, but the guy standing in front of me doesn't so much as crack a smile.

He watches me thoughtfully for a moment, those silver eyes darkening and slicing right through me. "You understand why we're here." It isn't a question.

"Of course she knows, Atlas," Gabriel chimes in.

"For me," I say anyway. My voice is flat, emotionless.

"Are you afraid?"

I almost laugh at the audacity of his question. "No. No, I'm super thrilled to have four strangers in my apartment for the sole reason of stealing my future." I clamp my mouth shut as stiffness ripples through my muscles, but it's too late. The words are out there.

Out of nowhere, the fourth guy appears in front of me, making me jump back in surprise. His hair is white, but what really catches my attention are the black ink tattoos covering his arms and what I can see of his chest from the black V-neck he's wearing. Vines of differing sizes wind around his left arm with thorns spaced along them and incredibly detailed roses, shaded in such a way they appear as if they're on fire. I've always wanted a tattoo, but I'm not sure what. That, and the idea of undergoing that amount of pain on purpose... I don't really understand it. Though I get the feeling that'd change after my first one.

"Perhaps not the *sole* reason," the tattooed vampire muses, and my eyes snap to his face just as his smoldering gaze trails the length of my body.

Heat floods my cheeks, and I stare at him, wide-eyed. I want to look away, to run far, but I have nowhere to go. I won't make it past these guys—I need to be smarter, which likely means I need them to think I've given up. At least for now.

"Don't freak the poor girl out, Lex," Kade says, pulling himself off the couch and approaching the small group we've made in the middle of my apartment.

My stomach feels heavy as my gaze bounces around the room. I bite the inside of my cheek to keep from saying something that definitely won't help my situation.

*I shouldn't be in this mess.*

These guys—these *vampires*—are here because my ancestors promised them the first-born female of their bloodline in exchange for saving their lives. To help them out of some shady, very much illegal business deal they got wrapped up in on Wall Street. Long story short, they sacrificed my life to save themselves, sealing the fate of an unborn girl before she even had a chance.

You'd think that might deter my great-grandparents or my grandparents or even my parents from having children. But no. In my mom's defense, she didn't know about the deal the Montgomery family made with the vampires until she was pregnant. My father kept it from her and prayed—like his father and grandfather did before him—that the child would be a boy.

When the doctor told my parents I was a girl, they were heartbroken. My mom was beside herself with anger—toward my dad and the cruelty of the fate her family had been given. They wanted to protect me, of course, but how were a couple of humans supposed to fight four hundred-or-so-year-old vampires? Any possibility would've been laughable at best. That's the problem with blood oaths. We are bonded on a level I'll never be able to outrun. Though that certainly isn't going to stop me from trying.

I moved to Washington, D.C. from New York City three

years ago, just shy of my twentieth birthday. I took a couple of years off after high school to travel the Pacific Northwest—and had the time of my life experiencing new places—before moving here to start my undergrad in Sociology at Georgetown University, courtesy of the guilt money my parents send to pay my tuition and rent. It's an unspoken agreement. They wire money into my account, and I live with knowing my own family sacrificed my freedom—and most likely my life—to these assholes.

Sociology piqued my interest after taking a very basic course in high school, and when it came time to decide the path for my future—even with how bleak I knew it would be—something in my gut told me this was the right choice. I'm almost halfway through my major and that hasn't changed—even though everything else about my life is about to now.

"We'll give you a few minutes to pack a bag," Atlas says, moving toward the kitchen and snatching a bright green apple from the bowl on the island. My best friend Brighton and I took a pottery class last year, and that uneven, lumpy bowl was my creation. Art in that form clearly isn't my forte. Atlas takes a loud bite and leans against the counter.

I watch him with a renewed sense of bitterness. "I'm not going anywhere with you. Not only am I pissed you showed up here in the middle of the fucking night, I'm in university. It's the first week of March—I can't just leave halfway through the term."

"That's what you're concerned about?" Lex asks with a sharp laugh, arching a dark brow at me. His brows are an odd contrast to his fair skin and white hair. "Humans truly are silly creatures."

Of course it's not my main concern, considering they are actively upending my life and I have absolutely no idea what's going to happen when we leave this place, but if I let any of that in even for a moment, I'm going to lose it. So I don't. Instead, I snap, "You might be concerned too if you were forking out sixty grand a year." He doesn't know it's not coming out of my pocket.

He shrugs. "You don't want to pack a bag, fine. I'll do it."

Before I can protest, he's gone in a blur of movement, causing a burst of air to blow my hair across my face. I tuck the dark brown waves back over my shoulder and glance around the room.

Kade grins at me when my gaze reaches him. "He's gonna go through your panty drawer."

I shake my head as exhaustion pulls at me. Evidently, the adrenaline is wearing off. "I don't care."

"We should go," Gabriel says from the couch, drumming his fingers along the back of it. "Calla's had a long night."

"Calla can speak for herself," I say in a sharp tone, though he's not wrong. I was tired when I left the campus library with Brighton. If my nerves weren't fried, I'd have likely passed out on the floor by now.

What I wouldn't give to open my eyes and realize all of this was a nightmare. No such luck. The vampires that broke into my apartment to kidnap me are very real, and I am very screwed.

When Kade steps toward me, my eyes narrow, and I immediately step back... right into Atlas's chest. *When did he move from the kitchen?*

I'm in no position to fight these guys, but my muscles tense as if I'm going to anyway.

Atlas snakes his arm around my waist before I can move. "Don't make this harder," he warns in a low voice, his lips brushing the shell of my ear.

I shiver, then try to drive my elbow back to get him to let go, but it does nothing but exert energy I'm already in low supply of.

"Calla." His voice makes me freeze, and I squeeze my eyes

shut. If this bastard thinks he's going to glamour me into compliance, he's got another thing coming.

I clench my fists tighter. "Let go of me."

"You don't need to keep fighting." With his free hand, he wraps his fingers around my throat, pushing gently until the back of my head rests against his chest.

The tension leaves my muscles, and I stop trying to break free of his hold. *What the fuck?*

"That's better," he murmurs against my hair, and his fingers slip away from my throat.

Confusion floods through me as I open my eyes to find Kade and Gabriel watching me. "W-what? No…"

Gabriel offers a faint smile. "Glamour works in different ways, angel. For vampires like Atlas, skin-to-skin contact is just as powerful as eye contact."

I shake my head as annoyance flickers through me. "That's not fair."

I think I feel a rumble of laughter against my back.

Lex walks down the hall from my bedroom, a duffle bag slung over his shoulder. His eyes shift between us, and he arches a brow. "We good?" Then he focuses on me. "Don't worry, I grabbed the pretty lace ones." He pats the side of the bag and winks at me.

"I'm going to kill you," I say in a low voice in an attempt to mask my shame; the fight in me is gone. "All of you." I pull away from Atlas, and he lets me. I walk to the door, grabbing my jacket and book bag off the hook before leaving my apartment. When I realize that I may never return, a pit of dread builds a home in my stomach.

## 2

They live in a fucking mansion in the Palisades. Because *of course* their house is in one of the most expensive neighborhoods in Washington.

It's at least three stories high and built into a hill, I realize as the Escalade slows to pull into the paved driveway. The light from inside gives the exterior a soft glow. Stone stairs lead up to the front door, and the massive exterior is made of glass and dark wood panels. The driveway is surrounded by a stone wall that frames the professionally maintained shrubbery and grass and is built taller to fit the height of the wood-paneled garage door. Tall trees surround the property, but not enough to block the curb appeal.

If it wasn't my very own prison, I might actually appreciate its luxury.

Atlas presses a button on the dash, opening the door, and we drive into an unnecessarily huge garage. The door closes soundlessly behind us as Atlas pulls into an empty spot between two other wildly expensive-looking cars. I'm vaguely aware when he kills the engine and the car doors start opening. The cold air seeps inside with the heat no longer blowing, and I shiver, tugging my jacket tighter around me as I peer around the garage from inside the quiet vehicle.

Being surrounded by concrete walls makes me want to bolt. It certainly doesn't help the sensation of being trapped, making it feel as if someone is standing on my chest. Even with the bright track lighting across the ceiling, the walls threaten to close in on me any second.

"Calla."

I flinch before turning to find my door open and Atlas standing there waiting for me to get out. I don't want to. My gaze drops to my lap where my hands are clenched into fists, and I let loose a faint sigh.

The passenger side door slams shut, and I jump, looking up in time to see the back of Kade's head before he disappears into the house with Lex not far behind him, my duffle bag slung over his shoulder.

I unbuckle my belt and reach down to grab my book bag off the floor, gripping it so tight my nails bite into my palm. I focus on that discomfort as I get out of the car to follow Atlas and Gabriel inside, my shoes echoing faintly on the concrete floor.

The shrill chirp of the car locking makes my pulse race, and I press my lips together when Gabriel rests his hand against my lower back.

"You're okay," he says and reaches past me to open the frosted glass door.

I walk into the house and am immediately greeted by warmth and a faint smell of lemon. This place is straight out of a Pottery Barn catalog. The walls at the back of the house are made entirely of floor-to-ceiling windows, which I imagine look absolutely stunning in daylight. The pool reflects the moonlight outside, and though I'm completely out of my element here, I can't help the twinge of excitement that flickers through me. *I've never lived anywhere with a pool.*

My eyes travel around the room, taking in the open-concept space. The furniture is... interesting. Nothing matches, yet somehow it works. There's a long maroon couch with a glass coffee table in front of it, stacked with books, and a few olive green and taupe chairs that complete the sitting area.

Beyond that is the kitchen. The counters are made up of two gray marble slab islands with a sink and stovetop built in. Dark wood cabinets provide storage below and match the tall cabinets built into the wall adjacent to the islands. The double oven built into the wall of cabinets looks professional enough to be in a Michelin star restaurant.

"You don't need to stand by the door," Kade says, leaning against one of the counters.

I blink, barely noticing that Gabriel is still at my side. "This place is ridiculous," I mumble, still taking it all in. Though I wouldn't mind taking advantage of that kitchen to make cookies or pastries. Maybe a cheesecake or some tarts. Baking has always been a hobby of mine, something to distract me when school gets overly stressful. Plus, I have an insane sweet tooth. There's hardly ever a time the cookie jar on the counter in my kitchen is empty.

Next to the kitchen is a full dining set with enough seating to fit a small army. It is also surrounded by windows.

"Evidently, sunlight isn't a concern," I comment in an absent tone as I walk further into the room.

"That's right," Lex confirms, dropping onto the couch and grabbing a book from the coffee table. He cracks it open as he kicks his feet up, then props a pillow under his head. "We don't burn... or sparkle, in case you were wondering."

I wasn't.

"I'll take you to your room and show you around on the way," Gabriel says from beside me.

"I don't need a tour of my glorified prison cell," I snap without a thought. As tired and defeated as I am, that fiery anger still rages on in me.

Lex whistles from behind his book, and it makes me want to throw something at him.

"You can have anything you want here," Kade says, pushing away from the counter to walk closer. My back stiffens in response to his proximity, but I don't move. "Anything at all. I certainly don't think you would receive the same in prison."

A muscle twitches in my jaw, a subtle reminder that if I continue clenching it this hard, I'm going to end up with a migraine. "I *want* to go home." My voice takes on a defiant tone, to which Kade smirks at.

"I do enjoy your sharp tongue."

"Fuck off, Kade," Lex says in a light tone without looking up from his book. "Give the girl a chance to get in the door before you start tormenting her."

Kade keeps his silver gaze on me a moment longer before sauntering away.

Atlas is gone too, I notice. I'm not sure when he disappeared—I was probably too enraptured by this insane house to pick up on his departure. I'm not sure what I was expecting—a stone castle in the middle of nowhere perhaps?—but a modern, mostly glass mansion wasn't it.

I lift my book bag onto my shoulder and sigh. "Let's go," I say, waiting for Gabriel to show me the way.

He leads me to a wide hallway off of the kitchen that I hadn't seen when we first walked in. The high ceilings leave ample room for the painted canvases hung on the otherwise plain white walls, and pot lights cast a golden glow down the hall. It leads to a second, more formal living room with a floor-to-ceiling fireplace and skylights. The dark gray furniture in this room all matches and appears to be more for show, not as though it's actually comfortable to sit on.

I follow Gabriel around a corner to a set of double doors. He opens one and gestures for me to walk in ahead of him. When I hesitate, he offers a faint smile that makes something flutter in my chest. Instead of trying to figure out what in the hell that is, I walk inside, and my mouth drops open.

This bedroom is in the corner of the house, so both outside walls are floor-to-ceiling windows that look out into the forest along the property. There's nothing but darkness to see right now, but I have a feeling the view during the day is nothing to scoff at. The queen bed faces the windows, and in the corner of the room is a gray lounge chair that matches the bedding, a gold free-standing lamp, and a small glass table with a vase of fresh white orchids.

*They know my favorite flower.*

A chill runs down my spine, and I hug my jacket closer as I'm reminded that these guys know way more about me than I know about them.

"It's pretty plain," Gabriel says. "If you want anything to personalize the space, let me know and I'll have it delivered. And there's a library in Atlas's office if you're looking for something to read. I know you enjoy books."

I bite the inside of my cheek, nodding silently. While I'm definitely curious about the aforementioned library, Gabriel knowing one of my favorite hobbies is yet another reminder of my current circumstances. I've always loved to read, though. And while I haven't had much time for reading anything aside from textbooks and assignments, that passion has stayed with me.

"There's a bathroom around there," Gabriel says softly,

pointing toward the break in the wall on the far side of the bed.

I set my book bag down next to where Lex left my duffle at the end of the bed and walk around to the wide-open bathroom. There looks to be a door that will slide across for privacy, and not only does it have his and hers vanities with sinks on opposite sides of the room, but two showers as well—and a soaker tub in between them.

My hand flies to my mouth when I catch my reflection in the mirror. I look like shit. Pale complexion, dark under-eye circles, and smeared eyeliner. Fair enough; I look as awful as I feel. Not to mention, my hair is a tangle of dark brown waves that could definitely use a wash; dry shampoo only lasts so long.

"Do you need a minute?"

I startle at the sound of Gabriel's voice and turn toward him. What I need is to get the hell out of here. Instead, I say, "Several."

He watches me for a moment before nodding toward a cabinet next to the vanity on the left. "There are towels and about a hundred different soaps and conditioners in there."

I arch a brow at him.

Gabriel shakes his head, but there's a fondness in his voice when he says, "Kade takes hair care very seriously."

Perhaps if the circumstances that landed me in this moment with Gabriel were different, I would smile.

He gives me one last look before heading out of the room. It's only once I hear the bedroom door click shut that I let out a breath. The next one gets caught in my throat, and I rush over to the shower and turn it on in hopes of covering the sound of the sob that tears its way up my throat. Tears spring in my eyes, and while I'm surprised at the sudden onslaught, I don't fight them back. I will let myself cry behind closed doors, but I will never let them see.

I strip out of my clothes, leaving them in a pile on the shiny marble floor, and step under the hot spray of water. My chin quivers as tears mix with water on my face, and I run my fingers through my hair until it's wet enough to lather with the glass bottle of eucalyptus and mint scented shampoo. *Stupid fancy soap.*

I scrub until my skin is an angry red, and by the time I'm rinsing the conditioner out of my hair, my belly aches and my temples are pounding. All I want to do is close my eyes and forget this entire night ever happened.

*I have to get out of here.*

My heavy limbs disagree, but it doesn't stop me from stepping out of the shower, leaving the water running, and quickly drying off. I wrap the towel around me and tiptoe into the bedroom to grab my duffel bag. I tear through it until I find a pair of leggings and a heavy beige sweater. I get changed as fast as I can and towel dry my hair enough I won't catch a cold the minute I step outside.

I grab my book bag with my cell phone and wallet and shove my feet into my shoes. My mind is going a million miles an hour, and I am very aware that what I'm about to attempt is ridiculously stupid, but I refuse to accept this as my reality—being stolen away from everything I love and for what? To be turned into a slave to four vampires? Nausea ripples through me, making my jaw clench as bile rises in my throat. I swallow hard and square my shoulders. I need to at least *try* to escape.

I shoulder my bag and go to the window near the bathroom. It takes up the entirety of the wall, but there's also a window panel that opens enough to get out—which is exactly what I do. I hold my breath as I unlatch the lock and push the panel open. I peek down and cringe. It's still a few feet, but much better than it could've been if they'd stuck me in a bedroom on the second or third floor.

Their mistake.

I climb out, my breath fogging the air in front of me as the cold knocks the wind out of my lungs. I suck in a deep breath and dart toward the line of trees along the side of the house which, to my benefit, is made of actual walls instead of windows.

My heart rattles in my chest as I sprint through the forest, tripping over fallen branches here and there, but managing to catch my balance before eating the ground each time. When I finally reach the road, I don't stop. I follow the asphalt until it meets the main road, then I pull my phone out and order a ride, choosing a meeting place a short distance away so I can keep moving.

I round the corner and see the license plate of my driver. I run the rest of the way down the sidewalk and throw myself into the back of the car, my chest heaving with every breath.

"You okay there, hon?" Leanne, my five-star driver asks, eyeing me from the rearview mirror. She has dark corkscrew curls that reach her shoulders, and she's wearing one of those puffy jackets in a bright yellow color. I can't really make out her expression in the dark, but her tone is kind.

"Yes," I force out. "Please just drive."

When she reads my address aloud to confirm the drop-off, my pulse races. I'd put in my home address just to get picked up.

"No," I say quickly. "I can't go there."

She frowns at me. "Are you sure you're all right? Should I call the police?"

I choke on a desperate laugh. *Unless the police can arrest four vampires for taking what they believe to be rightfully theirs based on a century-old blood oath, you'd be wasting a call, Leanne.*

"Hon?"

"No," I repeat. "I'm fine. Just head toward Pennsylvania Ave."

"I'm supposed to get an address," she says.

"I'll pay you whatever you want. In cash."

She doesn't hesitate this time. We pull away from the curb, heading toward the interstate, and I can't help but feel as though I'm fighting a losing battle.

## 3

The streets of Washington are quiet, unlike the pounding in my chest. My head is spinning and my forehead is damp with sweat. I have no idea what I'm doing, and every second I don't figure it out, I'm losing what little ground I managed to gain on these guys.

The driver keeps looking at me in the rearview mirror; I'm freaking her out.

I'm also putting her in danger. Who knows what the guys will do if they find me with another person?

Panic spikes as I reach for the door handle. "Let me off here," I say, quickly pulling a fifty-dollar bill out of my bag.

She pulls over and hits the brakes as I toss the bill at her. "Wait—"

"Thanks," I mutter, getting out of the car and slamming the door shut before I take off down the street.

My chest is tight as my heart pounds in time with my shoes hitting the pavement. My lungs sting from the exertion and the cold air, but I don't stop. I clutch the phone in my hand, and before I'm even aware of what I'm doing, I've dialed Brighton's number. I chew my lip as the line rings and rings… and rings. Finally, there's a click, and my stomach sinks.

"Calla! Where the hell are you?" Brighton shouts, and I immediately pull the phone away from my ear. Music blares in the background, and I cringe.

I've stopped running so I'm not too out of breath to speak, but I'm still moving at a fast pace. I need to put as much distance between me and them as I can. "Brighton… can you hear me?"

"Hello?" She's still shouting. "Hang on! I'm going outside!" A minute later, the music quiets and the line is silent. "Shit, okay. What's up, lady?"

"I need a favor." A car honks in the distance, and I jump, whipping my head around to find the street and sidewalk behind me empty. I start walking faster.

"At almost two in the morning?" she asks with a short laugh. "What are you up to? Oh god, please don't tell me you went home to keep studying and you want me to bring you caffeine."

"I need your credit card," I blurt. If I use mine, I have to assume they'll track it. But maybe if I go to a building filled with people, I can hide for a short time. It's dangerous to stop, knowing they could come for me, but I need to rest, to come up with a better plan than just running until I can't any longer. If things had gone the way I'd imagined when thinking of this awful moment, I would've killed those vampires before I had an opportunity to know their names. It was a naive thought, and I hate that it was my only real strategy, because now I'm pretty well screwed. "Actually, I need you to book me a room at the Four Seasons."

"Uhhh." Her voice cracks. "Calla—"

"Please, Bri. I can't explain anything right now, but I need a place."

"Why don't you crash at mine? I'll be home soon, and we can talk about what's going on."

"No," I say quickly. I can't lead them to her. I'm not about to put my best friend in the path of four vampires who are likely pretty pissed I gave them the slip in their own home. "Please just get me a room."

There's a short pause before Brighton says, "Calla, you know I'm here for you no matter what. If you're in trouble—"

I cut her off, rushing to say, "I don't have time to fill you in." I'm not even sure what the hell I'd tell her, anyway.

She sighs. "Hang on."

I stay on the line for a couple of minutes, nibbling on the pad of my thumb as I peek over my shoulder every ten seconds. Waiting for them to come after me, to find me.

"Calla?"

My pulse jackhammers momentarily. "Yeah, I'm here."

"The suite is booked under my name for as long as you need. I sent the confirmation to your email. If there are any issues, call me."

I let out a breath. "Thank you, Brighton. Seriously. I owe you."

"Just... whatever is going on, please be careful. And promise you'll fill me in as soon as you can?"

"I'll talk to you soon," I say, disconnecting before I tell her another lie. Honestly, I'm not sure when I'll speak to her next. I just need to make it somewhere safe so I can figure out my next move.

Do Atlas, Kade, Gabriel, and Lex already know I'm gone? I think it's safe to say yes. Can they track me to the hotel? There's a good chance of that if my theory of hiding among a bunch of other people is wrong, which it very likely could be. But if I can barricade myself in a room just long enough to come up with a less awful plan than run and hide, then maybe—just maybe—I can get myself out of this.

The first thing I do when I get into the suite is lock the door and shove the heavy coffee table against it before checking the windows. I'm on the top floor, so it's a little ridiculous, but I do it anyway. Anything to feel a semblance of safety—of control.

I kick off my shoes and pace the fancy room, my stocking feet padding soundlessly across the dark wood floor. I'm not sure what made Brighton spring for a suite with a full living room and dining area, but I'm not going to complain. Considering she knows as well as I do that it'd take me all semester to pay her back for this, and she did it without asking a million questions that I can't answer right now. Though, knowing Brighton as well as I do, she didn't think twice about dropping this kind of money. I suppose that comes with being as well-off as her family is.

I pull in slow, deep breaths, trying to wrack my brain for a plan that isn't absolutely insane. I pull my phone out and scroll through my contacts. My finger hovers over my mom's number, but I shake my head and sigh, tossing the phone onto the marble dining table. As sympathetic to my plight as she may be, there isn't a thing she can do. And my dad… The man isn't brave—or stupid—enough to go against the vampires his great-grandparents sealed my fate with.

I briefly consider what would happen if I went back to New York, but it's pointless. Even if my parents wanted to protect me, two humans against four vampires wouldn't stand a chance. And as much as I resent my family—my father mostly—for this life, I couldn't do that to them.

After I've changed out of my clothes and wrapped myself in the plush bathrobe, I pull my hair into a messy bun on the top of my head and brush my teeth using the complimentary disposable brush I found in the bathroom. All the while trying to avoid my reflection in the mirror.

I rinse out my mouth and exhale slowly before walking out of the bathroom.

A scream tears its way up my throat when my eyes land on Atlas, lounging in the wingback chair in the corner of the bedroom. Something in me—survival instincts maybe—kicks in, and I race toward the door. The table I had pushed in front of it is back where it was when I arrived. *What the hell?* I barely get the door open an inch before Atlas reaches past me and slams it shut. He grabs me by the shoulders and turns me around to face him. My back hits the closed door, and I immediately start fighting him.

"You want to do this again?" he asks with a subtle head tilt.

"Fuck you," I snap, but cease shoving at his chest for a moment to catch my breath.

His eyes roam my face before dropping to my chest where my robe has fallen open. His gaze freezes there, and the air leaves my lungs.

"Kade wanted to come get you," he says in a low voice, his eyes hooded. He's so close I could count his dark lashes. You know, if I wasn't preoccupied with trying to get away from him.

I swallow past the dryness in my throat. "So why are *you* here then?" I force out.

"Be glad it's me, Calla." His eyes finally lift back to my face as he reaches forward and closes my robe. "He was keen on punishing you for running away."

I wet my lips, tipping my head back against the door so I can meet his gaze. "And you?"

He shakes his head. "What I'd like to do to you…"

"You're going to kill me," I say in a flat voice. It's the only conclusion I've come to. No matter what happens, these men will be my end.

Atlas blinks at me. His eyes are dark but there's something else in them. He looks tired. "I'm not here to kill you."

"Doesn't mean it won't happen," I say, my throat suddenly thick with emotion. "You may not even mean to do it—any of you—but it will happen."

His expression remains impassive. "You're so convinced we're monsters."

"Aren't you?" I whisper.

He purses his lips in thought for a moment. "Perhaps to some." He leans in and brushes his fingers along my cheek. "But not you."

My jaw clenches against his hand as confusion floods through me. "Then let me go," I plead, holding his gaze. "Tell the others you couldn't find me. I'll get on a plane and—"

He drops his hand, and my skin tingles where he was touching. "We will find you wherever you run. When are you going to realize that?"

I grab the front of his shirt without thinking, wrinkling the soft cotton material between my fingers. "Why? What could you possibly want from me? You've essentially ruined my life, stolen my future, and for what?"

He peers down at where I'm white-knuckling his shirt before meeting my gaze again. "We've waited a long time for you, Calla."

I shake my head, my brows tugging together. "That doesn't answer my question."

"It's not a simple one."

A shiver runs through me, and I swallow hard when I catch a flash of his elongated canines. "You're going to feed on me," I say, my voice barely above a whisper. What else could they want me for besides a personal human vending machine?

His eyes shift between mine, but he doesn't miss a beat. "Yes." Again he leans in until his lips are next to my ear, his breath tickling the skin below my earlobe. "What's more, you'll enjoy every second of it."

I suck in a breath when he presses his mouth to the pulse at my neck. His tongue darts out and flicks against my skin, and my head swims. I grip his shirt tighter, though I'm not sure if it's to pull him closer or shove him away. His proximity—and ridiculously powerful pheromones—are messing with my head something fierce, and I despise that they affect me so much even though I want to kill him. Because that's the only way I can see out of this—it's either me or them.

Then Atlas steps back, and I let go. A flush creeps across my cheeks, and I look away, suddenly embarrassed by the heat pooling in my belly. I quickly walk toward the sitting area, wanting to put some distance between us so I can think clearly.

"You shouldn't be embarrassed about your response to me. Or feel shy about what your body desires, for that matter," Atlas says, following me and lowering himself into one of the chairs.

"I have no idea what you're talking about," I lie. "I'm sleep-deprived, that's all."

"With how tightly wound you are, I'd say you're more than *sleep*-deprived."

I choke on a forced laugh. "You don't know anything about me."

Those silver eyes pierce right through me. "Care to make a bet on that?"

"Not a chance," I say around a yawn.

"Because you know you're wrong."

"Oh yeah?" I cross my arms, leaning against the back of the chair. "What do you know about me, Atlas?"

He's out of his chair and leaning over mine in the time it

takes me to blink. I suck in a short breath as he grips the armrests and leans in until his nose is an inch from mine. I'm not sure I'll ever get used to the incredible speed these vampires possess.

"You think we haven't spent years getting to know you?" His breath tickles my cheek, and I force myself to hold his gaze. "That we haven't memorized everything about your life while we waited for the right moment to—"

"Ruin it?" I interject with a bitter tone.

His eyes seem to darken, and he lowers his voice. "You think I don't know how to set your body off like a fucking firecracker with a single touch?" There's a challenge in his voice that has my pulse pounding beneath my flushed skin.

Boldness grips me, and I say, "Then why haven't you?"

He stares at me for a long moment without saying anything, and then he murmurs, "Because Kade called first dibs on your pussy."

Those words feel like ice water being dumped on me, effectively murdering the fluttering in my stomach.

I scowl and shove him away. "Asshole."

Atlas straightens and walks toward the door. "Get some sleep. You'll be returning to our place tomorrow. And Calla," he says, pausing to look at me over his shoulder, "don't run again. It won't be me coming to get you next time, and Kade isn't nearly as patient as I am."

I stare straight ahead until the door clicks shut behind him. And then a rush of tears blurs my vision as I stand and walk into the bedroom, crawling into the massive bed. Exhaustion clings to every part of me, which is the only thing that allows sleep to pull me under.

I dream of razor-sharp teeth. Blood everywhere. A pounding in my chest and... a throbbing between my thighs.

My eyes fly open to a dark room, and for a moment, I

forget. A fleeting, peaceful moment before it's all ripped away and reality settles in once again.

I shoot up in the bed, clutching my chest as it all comes rushing back.

"Good morning."

I yelp before slapping a hand over my mouth. My head whips toward the voice, and when my eyes meet Kade's silver ones, I scramble off the bed, Atlas's voice ringing in my head.

*Kade called first dibs on your pussy.*

I back away from the bed, keeping my eyes on him. He leans back against the headboard, stretching his black jean-clad legs out on the white duvet. My breath catches when he flicks his tongue along his bottom lip before smirking.

"Kade," I whisper, my voice shakier than I'd like. I clear my throat. "What are you doing here? What time is it?" I glance toward the window. The sunrise is barely skimming the sky, so it can't be much later than six.

I shift my gaze back to the bed, but he's not there. The hair on the back of my neck sticks up, and I hold my breath. "Kade…"

"Turn around." His voice makes me freeze; he's right behind me. He's not glamouring me, but I do what he says anyway.

I stare at his chest as the seconds tick past. Finally, I force my gaze to his face. He's clean-shaven today and smells annoyingly good. Like peppermint and expensive cologne, as if he took a shower before coming here. And his dark brown waves are tousled stylishly and frame his face in a way that makes him look as if he should be on a runway during New York Fashion Week instead of in this hotel room with me.

His lips curl into a grin. "Good morning," he says again, reaching forward and capturing a piece of hair that escaped my bun while I slept. He twirls it around his finger, before tucking it behind my ear. My skin tingles where he touches, but I don't move away.

"Hi," I say in a quiet voice.

"Hi," he echoes with a sparkle in his eyes. "How did you sleep?"

"Does it matter?"

Kade frowns briefly. "Of course." His eyes flick between mine, evaluating. "You're exhausted." He looks past me toward the bed. "You should go back to sleep for a while."

"I'm fine," I say automatically.

He stares at me as silence stretches between us. "Calla—"

"Don't," I cut him off. "You came here to drag me back to that house. Let's just go." I take a step toward the door, but Kade wraps his fingers around my wrist and pulls me back. Before I know what's happening, he presses a soft kiss against my cheek.

I blink at him as warmth fills my face. "What was that for?"

He shrugs. "I wanted to do that when I crawled into bed next to you an hour ago, but I figured it would be better to wait until you were awake."

"Kidnapping is completely fine, but you draw the line at kissing while the other person is unconscious? Good to know."

Kade chuckles, sliding his fingers through mine and tracing his thumb back and forth across my skin. "Yes, I'd very much like for you to be awake while I ravish you." He licks his lips, leaning closer. "I think you'd like that too."

I'm shaking my head, but my body is saying something else entirely.

"Say it," he taunts. "Tell me you don't want it."

I narrow my eyes at him and try to pull my hand away, but he grips it tighter.

"Tell me, Calla."

"And if I don't?" I challenge. I have no idea what's come over me, but every nerve ending in my body wants Kade's attention. Craves it. It's dangerous and is likely going to get me killed, but I can't deny the way it excites me. *Screw my body for betraying me.* The rational part of me understands that mostly has to do with the lure a vampire has over humans, which is typically how they capture their prey. But it's more difficult than I expected to ignore it. Maybe because there's a part of me that knows this whole thing would be easier if I just... let it happen. If only my stubborn nature could accept that.

He pulls me forward into his chest and clasps the side of my neck with his other hand, using his thumb to hold my jaw and keep me in place. "If you don't," he says slowly, "I'm going to make you come on my fingers. Then with my tongue. And then, if you're a good girl, I might give you my cock."

My eyes pop wide. I'm not a virgin by any means. I fooled around with a couple of different guys my first year of university, but I'm certainly not used to... *this*.

Kade smirks at my response—or lack thereof. "Let me take care of you," he murmurs, brushing his nose along mine.

My heart is in my throat as I lean into him until our lips touch. Once. Twice. I close my eyes and press my mouth against his fully. Kade slips his hand away from my neck and pulls my hair out of the messy bun. Dark brown waves cascade over my shoulders, and he buries his fingers in them, tilting my head back slightly to deepen the kiss. I grip the front of his shirt, my heart racing as I remember that the only thing keeping Kade from my body is the bathrobe I fell asleep in.

Without warning, he slips the hand he had entwined with mine free and slides it into my robe. When his fingers brush the skin above my belly button, I gasp into his mouth. They slide up between my breasts, opening the front of the robe wider as he parts my lips with his tongue. Our lips move against each other while he cups my breast, using his thumb and finger to roll my nipple into a hard pebble.

I groan against his lips. "Kade…"

He breaks the kiss, pinching my nipple as he leans back just enough to look me in the eyes. His eyes are filled with liquid fire, hooded and glimmering with the promise of so much pleasure it's making my knees weak. He holds my gaze as he trails his hand back down my chest to my stomach and then lower. I hold my breath as his fingers dance across my skin, slowing to a stop when he reaches the apex of my thighs.

My breathing turns shallow as he tilts my head to the side and presses his mouth against my neck. And when his fingers start moving between my legs, my head swims with lust.

He traces my lips and drags a single finger up the length of my slit before dipping into me.

I bite my lip hard to keep from moaning.

"Fuck," Kade growls against my skin. "I want to drive my cock into you so hard you won't be able to walk." He bites my neck playfully, his fangs retracted so he doesn't break the skin. "But I'm going to take it slow and enjoy how fucking amazing you feel against my fingers." His thumb lands on my clit, and I gasp. He moves it in slow circles, teasing while he pushes his finger inside me.

"Oh my god," I breathe, grabbing his shoulder to steady myself.

"You're already so wet for me." He kisses up my neck and along my jaw until our mouths meet once again.

"Shut up," I pant against his lips as he adds a second finger and applies pressure to my clit until I'm seeing stars.

Kade grabs my free hand and presses it against his crotch. "It's only fair, considering you've got me rock solid."

I sigh into his mouth as heat ripples through me and kiss him harder, palming the front of his pants until he growls.

In a blur of motion, he lifts me up and carries me to the bed without removing his fingers from between my thighs. My head hits the soft duvet, and Kade leans over me, continuing his ministrations while I writhe beneath him. His teeth scrape the delicate skin at my throat, and my heart slams against my ribcage.

When he hits a particularly sensitive spot inside me, my hips vault off the mattress. He pulls back and smirks before pinning me to the bed with his arm over my waist. I roll my hips, urging him to go deeper, and he quickly obliges, picking up speed as he pumps in and out of me.

My eyes roll back and I grip the sheets on either side of me as my body climbs to new heights of ecstasy.

"Keep going," I say breathlessly.

Kade closes his mouth around my neck, nipping and sucking, swirling his tongue against my skin. My nerves short-circuit. *Fuck*. I want him to bite me.

I tilt my head to the side, providing the invitation as my body vibrates beneath him. "Kade." My voice trembles with a twisted mix of fear and desire. I'm afraid to want this.

He responds by curling his fingers inside me, hitting a new spot that feels so fucking good. I whimper, lifting my hips as much as I can to push him deeper.

"Oh fuck," I moan.

"Come for me," he murmurs against my neck, circling my clit harder, faster.

His words launch me off the edge, and a wickedly powerful orgasm whips through me like a wildfire of pleasure.

"That's it," he purrs, sliding his hand up my chest to wrap his fingers around my throat. "Ride my fingers."

I roll my hips, groaning as he holds his fingers still inside me as I move against them.

"Good girl," he praises, then kisses me hard as I ride the aftershocks of my orgasm. He slides his fingers out slowly, making me shiver and jump when he flicks my clit with a devilish grin on his lips.

When he pulls back and licks his fingers, my stomach pools with heat. *Holy shit.* I'm still catching my breath, but my body already wants more of him. One orgasm from Kade, and I feel as though it would be dangerously easy to become addicted.

And that really doesn't bode well for my escape.

## 4

We head back to the house once I get dressed. I didn't bring any of my clothes when I took off last night, so I'm stuck wearing the deep blue dress Kade brought me. I slip into the bathroom to get changed and pull on black stockings before grabbing my book bag and leaving the suite with Kade.

I still have no idea how I'm going to explain last night to Brighton, but that's the least of my problems right now.

The ride back to the house is quiet, and when we walk inside, Lex and Gabriel are waiting in the living room. *Great.*

Lex has his nose in a book but glances up when the door to the garage closes behind us. "Look what we have here. Little girl lost found her way home," he says with a wink in my direction.

I shake my head. "What?"

"Perhaps we should get you a leash."

His playful tone grinds on my nerves, and my pulse ticks faster. "Perhaps you should—"

"Coffee is fresh," Gabriel cuts in as he stands from the couch and walks toward the kitchen. "Calla?"

My gaze follows him across the space that looks even more massive in daylight. "Yeah," I finally say, choosing to ignore Lex completely.

In the kitchen, Gabriel hands me a steaming mug of coffee. "You drink it black, right?"

I nod. "Um, thanks." Taking a small sip, I almost moan at the taste. *Of course, their coffee is amazing.* I shouldn't be bitter about it. If anything, I suppose I should be grateful. I'm stuck here for the foreseeable future, but at least the coffee's good.

Out of nowhere, I find myself asking, "Why am I here?"

Gabriel leans against the counter. "You belong to us, Calla."

I swallow my immediate snarky retort and instead ask, "To what end?"

Lex lowers his book and glances over at us. "Yours, I suppose," he answers with a wink—he does that a lot.

My stomach churns as panic creeps in, making my muscles feel heavy.

"The agreement becomes void upon your natural death," Gabriel says. "We also have the option to terminate it."

*Which will never happen.* The words are implied. So my life, whatever future I might have seen for myself, is effectively over.

"Don't look so hopeless, angel," Gabriel says, and I glance at him to find his eyes filled with... compassion? No, that must be a trick. He offers a faint smile before leaving me standing in the kitchen by myself. He disappears around the corner, and I hear faint footsteps climb the stairs to the second level I haven't seen yet. I guess Gabriel has no desire to finish giving me a tour of the house.

I jump when Lex tosses the book onto the coffee table and gets up, coming into the kitchen. When he starts pulling food out of the fridge, I slide out of the way.

As Lex cooks breakfast, the house fills with the savory

aroma of eggs and bacon, and despite my desire to flee this place, my stomach rumbles. Because I'm human and need food to survive—and I'm freaking starving.

Kade pulls a barstool over from the dining room and sits at one of the kitchen islands as he scrolls through his phone. I try to ignore it when I feel his eyes on me, but I can't shake the memory of his touch.

I take a long drink of my coffee and walk to the fridge. I pull out a plastic container of strawberries and blueberries, turning to the sink to rinse them off.

Lex flips the sizzling bacon and glances in my direction. "Hungry?"

I nod, plopping a blueberry in my mouth. "So you guys eat human food then."

Kade chuckles, setting his phone on the counter. "Yes, Calla. We eat like normal people. Well, most of us. Only born vampires don't need human food to survive—just blood."

"So turned vampires can survive on either?"

"We need both," Lex chimes in, cracking an egg into a frying pan before scrambling it with the spatula in his hand.

"Are all of you turned then?"

Lex and Kade exchange a glance that I almost miss.

"What? Is that some sort of secret?"

Before either can answer, Atlas walks in from the back of the house. Apparently one of the windows is actually a door that I hadn't noticed last night.

His hair is damp and the front of his light gray shirt is darkened with sweat. It dawns on me at that moment I didn't work out this morning. It's the first time in... I can't even recall how long that I missed one. The thought makes me frown, and I take another sip of coffee.

Atlas stops at the counter and grabs a strawberry from the container in front of me. His gaze lands on me, holds for a moment, and then shifts to where Kade is scrolling through his phone again. His brow arches briefly as if he *knows* what we did at the hotel this morning, and my cheeks fill with heat. I try to cover my face by taking another sip of coffee, but the moment passes without comment, and relief pours through me as he leaves the kitchen.

I'm not sure what causes me to set my mug down and go after him up the staircase to the second level, but I do. Yeah, I'm hungry, but I need answers more than I need food right now.

I follow the brightly lit hallway, taking in the abstract art hung along the white walls until I find an open door near the end. Either Atlas didn't hear me come after him, or he didn't bother to wait for me to catch up.

My breath halts when I step into the last room at the end of the hall—the only door slightly open—and find Atlas completely naked. Every inch of his golden-toned body looks as if it's been etched by gods, which is about as infuriating as it is attractive. I can't help but let my gaze wander...

"Shit, sorry." I whip around so I'm no longer looking at it —*him*. Instead, I try to focus on the room. The dark gray walls, blank of any art or other decor. The entire room actually is very plain. It suits him.

"Did you need something?" His voice is level, as if he's unbothered by my barging into his room and him being on display.

"Uh, yeah. I mean not right now, while you're... I just... I have questions."

"Calla." His voice is closer. "You don't need to hide."

I slowly turn around, forcing my gaze level with his. The heat from his body makes me want to retreat, but I keep still. "I—"

"Have questions. That you need to think very hard before you ask, because you may not be prepared for the answers."

I cross my arms, glancing past him toward the giant four-poster bed in the corner of the room. It's a mountain of black pillows and sheets that look silk from where I'm standing, and I can't help but imagine what I might feel like to—*no*. I need to focus. I look back at Atlas. "I deserve to know what's going on."

"That's not what I said."

I arch a brow. "Then what are you saying?"

"That it would be a lot easier if you kept those questions to yourself."

"Easier for *you*," I remark in a snippy tone. I may be stuck here, but that doesn't mean I'm going to sit quietly.

"For you too, I'd suspect," he muses. "Now, if you don't mind, I'd like to shower."

"I do mind," I snap, surprising myself. I'm sick of the aloof act from him.

"Are you planning to join me then?" His expression is smooth, serious. "You can ask all the questions you want."

I stare at him. I have to assume he's being serious because that's the only side I've seen to this guy, but I can't bring myself to say yes.

Atlas shrugs. "Lost your chance." He walks across the room and slides open a frosted glass door to an en suite bathroom. A moment later, the shower turns on, and I walk out of the room with a knot in my stomach.

Backtracking, I return to the kitchen, though I am definitely not hungry anymore. I stop at the fridge and grab a bottle of water, downing half of it before I close the door and look to where Lex and Kade are sitting in the dining room, devouring plates full of bacon and eggs. When I approach the table and drop into an empty seat, they both turn to look at me, and a frown tugs at my lips when I realize they heard the conversation between Atlas and me.

"Where's Gabriel?" I ask to quickly fill the silence.

"He left for work," Lex says, gulping down a glass of orange juice.

I nod, reaching for the dish of strawberries because I know I should put something in my stomach. I bite into one and ask, "What does he do?" My tone is curious, though it's mostly for show. They seem to know everything about me, and I'm going to have to figure them out if I have any chance at making it through this *arrangement* alive.

Kade shrugs, then with a smirk says, "I don't actually know."

Lex rolls his eyes and tosses a blueberry in his mouth. "That's because you don't pay attention to anything."

"That's not true." His smirk grows as he turns his attention to me. "Isn't that right, Calla?"

I glare at him. "You did not just say that."

His smirk remains. "Oh, come on."

"You should eat something."

I jump at the sound of Atlas's voice behind me. He pulls out the chair next to me and sits before scooping a pile of scrambled eggs onto the plate in front of me.

"Lex ate all the bacon," Kade comments, pulling his phone out.

Atlas ignores him, angling himself toward me. "Eat."

"Fuck off," I shoot back. "I'm not a child."

A muscle feathers along his jaw and a drop of water falls from a strand of hair in his face, wetting the front of his light gray T-shirt. He catches my gaze, and my mouth goes dry. "You're going to eat what I put on your plate and you're not going to argue with me about it. Understood?"

I'm nodding before I can stop myself. Except, I wouldn't be able to stop myself if I tried. *Fucking glamour*. I pick up the fork next to my plate and start eating.

After a few minutes of eating in silence, I glance toward Lex. "Do the rest of you have jobs?"

Lex nods. "I'm a kindergarten teacher."

I almost choke on my eggs when my head whips toward him—only to find him smirking at me. "Funny," I deadpan.

"Hey. I'm great with kids."

"That's terrifying to even think about," I mutter, returning my gaze to the plate in front of me.

"He works for me," Atlas says in a smooth voice before taking a drink of his coffee.

"Best boss ever," Lex remarks dryly, but Atlas's expression doesn't change.

"Doing what?" It's a simple question, but it has the potential to unlock a door to the past I'm not sure I'm really ready to open. Because whatever they do is tied to the reason I'm stuck here. To this day, I don't know how they saved my great-great-grandfather, just that whatever went down in New York could easily have cost him everything, including his life. When you're dealing with shady businesspeople, nothing is off the table.

"Boring communications shit," Lex answers, and I decide to leave it at that. For now.

"I'm a model," Kade chimes in, "though you could probably have guessed that."

I arch a brow at him. "And a humble one at that." My sarcastic tone seems to please him because he's grinning even as he continues to scroll on his phone. "Seriously, though. What do you guys do all day when you're not kidnapping university students?"

Lex snorts. "We typically travel a lot for work. Between Washington and New York City mostly."

"Right," I say, "and what exactly does that entail?" I ask before adding, "If I'm going to be here a while, I think it's fair that I get to know something about you guys."

"What about us makes you think we're fair?" Kade challenges, flicking his gaze in my direction.

"I just… Fine. Tell me something else then. Anything."

"We built this house," Lex says. "Atlas designed it."

My eyes widen. "Wow." I can't help but sound impressed—I am.

"Yep. It's a pretty fancy prison, don't you think?"

I shoot him a glare, but choose not to respond to that comment and instead say, "So Atlas designs stuff. What do you like to do?"

Lex shrugs. "I like pain."

I blink at him. "I don't…" My eyes go to his tattoos; I have to assume that's what he's talking about because the alternatives are just too creepy to consider. "Oh. That's… cool."

"Do you have any tattoos?" Kade asks.

I'm still admiring Lex's when I say, "Pretty sure you know that I don't."

Kade chuckles. "Fair point, though if they were on your back…" He trails off, and I roll my eyes.

"I don't have any tattoos," I reply in a firm voice.

Atlas remains silent through the whole exchange, drinking his coffee as if the rest of us aren't even there.

When I finish the food on my plate, I down a glass of orange juice and push my chair back. "Do I need to ask permission to leave the table, or do I still have *some* free will around here?" I direct the question at Atlas—he seems to be the one the others look to—and hold my chin high when he glances at me.

"Watch it," he warns.

I cross my arms. "You four have been watching me for god knows how long. You'd think you would have learned enough about me to know I'm not going to make this easy for you. You want a quiet, complacent human to boss around and bite?" I shiver at the last part, but quickly continue, "You chose the wrong person."

Lex rolls his eyes. "Well, we didn't just *pick* you."

I get up and step away from the table, very aware of the three pairs of eyes on me. "Yeah, well, you still chose to take me. I'm betting there was nothing in that agreement you made with my family that forced you to ruin my life, and yet here we are."

"You're being narrow-minded," Kade says in an agitated tone. "Have you considered that this arrangement could be a good thing?"

I belt out a laugh. "Don't fucking kid yourself. This *arrangement* is a death sentence. Four vampires and a single human in one house? Wonder how that's going to turn out." Maybe I haven't looked at it that way before, but the moment the bitter words leave my lips, my pulse spikes, and I'm moving backward.

"Calla—" Atlas starts.

"No." My voice cracks, and I cringe inwardly. "I... need to study." I need something *normal*.

Before they can say anything more, I grab my book bag and hurry out of the room. I don't stop until I'm in the bedroom Gabriel showed me to last night, with the door shut and locked. It's an almost laughable notion, that a simple lock could keep them out, but I do it anyway.

I glance toward the bed, kicking off my Docs near the door before I get into it. The sheets are so soft it makes me angry. I'm aware the feeling is a little ridiculous, but I can't shake it. I don't want to feel comfortable here—I want to leave.

With a heavy sigh, I lean against the massive collection of pillows at the headboard and pull out my textbooks. I toss the empty bag to the end of the bed and sigh to the empty room before cracking open my sociology book. I'm probably not in the right headspace to study, but at this point, I'll try just about anything to keep my mind off my very fucked up reality—for as long as I can.

## 5

By mid-afternoon, I'm tired of being cooped up in the bedroom—as fancy as it is—so I take my textbook outside and sit by the pool.

Being the beginning of March means the air is still cold, but I don't mind it. The sky is clear and the sun is shining, reflecting some heat off the pool, while the breeze is clearing my head and, surprisingly, allowing me to focus on the words in front of me. I can pretend, at least for a few fleeting moments, that I'm not a prisoner here.

I uncap my pen and underline a section of the text, jotting down a quick note in the margin.

My gaze lifts when Gabriel walks around the side of the house from the front. I press my lips together as I take him in, dressed impeccably in a navy suit, though his tie is pulled away from the collar of his white dress shirt and he's carrying the jacket over his arm. His copper hair gleams in the sun as he approaches, offering me a smile, and lowers himself onto the lounge chair next to me.

"How's it going?" He glances at the textbook in my lap. "Doing a little light reading, I see."

"Studying," I tell him, though he probably guessed that. "How was work? You're not secretly the President or something, are you?"

Gabriel laughs. "Where did you get that idea?"

I shrug, clicking my pen. "We are in Washington, and look at you."

"A lot of people wear suits here," he points out. "You're right in that I do work in politics."

"Do you work for the White House?"

His silver eyes sparkle with amusement. "I can't talk a lot about what I do for security reasons, but no, I don't work at the White House."

"That's a shame. I binged *Scandal* for a third time last semester. It's one of my favorites."

He nods as if he's following along, but then says, "That's a television show?"

I bite my tongue to keep from spilling about the entire show because we'd be sitting here all day, and instead say, "Uh, yeah."

Gabriel seems to pick up that I'm not going to elaborate and looks back at my textbook, tilting his head to read the cover. "Are you enjoying your program?"

"Some of it is pretty dry, but overall I am. My gut tells me I made the right choice going into sociology. Not that I have any idea of what I'll do when I graduate." My chest tightens at the thought. I don't even know what's going to happen tomorrow let alone two years from now. *If I'll even make it to graduation.*

"What made you pick Georgetown?"

"Honestly, the city. My mom took me on a trip here when I was in high school, and I sort of fell in love with it. So when it came time to start applying to schools, Georgetown was my top pick. I knew I couldn't stay in New York"—I also knew it wouldn't have mattered where I went, they would have tracked me down—"and I'm happy this is where I ended up." I frown. "I mean Washington, not *here* specifically."

He smiles faintly. "I knew what you meant, angel."

I nod, then take the lull in conversation to change the topic. "You know, the others aren't very forthcoming with information," I tell him, glancing at my lap. "You all know everything about me, but the moment I start asking questions..." I shake my head and turn toward him. "I don't want to be here. That isn't news. But the least you could do is tell me what's going to happen to me and *why* I'm here, because the fact that you all own me isn't an explanation."

"I understand you want to know, and there will be a time when things will become clear and make sense." The *but not right now* is left unsaid, which almost makes it worse.

"I'm not a pet, Gabriel," I snap. "I'm not just along for the ride. I have a life and friends, and I'm not going to just fall in line and play house with a bunch of vampires." My pulse ticks faster as I catch my breath from that little outburst.

He nods, standing from the lounge chair. "I'll speak with the others." He steps back, but before walking away he drapes his jacket over my shoulders.

I open my mouth, but no words come out. I'm overwhelmed by a woodsy citrus scent with a hint of fabric softener. My lips start to form a smile before I can stop myself, so it's a good thing Gabriel is already walking through the door to the house.

I finish reading and annotating one chapter and yawn. I close the cover and set it on the end of the lounge chair before swinging my legs over the side to stand. The superfancy coffee maker in the kitchen is calling my name like a siren; I could use a boost of caffeine.

The door to the house opens before I can get up, and Kade walks out—in bright red swim shorts.

I arch a brow at him as he approaches, his bare feet

soundless against the concrete. "You're not..." I trail off, glancing toward the pool. "It's March! You're going to freeze."

He stops at the back of my chair, leaning against it as he grins down at me. "It's a heated pool, Calla. Why do you think it's still open?"

"Okay, but—" I don't get a chance to finish my sentence before Kade walks past me and dives into the water.

I jump back when the water splashes, shaking my head at him. *Crazy bastard.*

Kade swims laps around the pool while I attempt to continue studying. It quickly becomes futile. I've read the same line at least three times, but the words aren't sticking. Not when I can feel the weight of Kade's gaze on me. With a sigh, I close my textbook and pull Gabriel's jacket off my shoulders, draping it over the back of the lounge chair before I stand. Inching toward the pool, I lock eyes with Kade.

"You coming in?" He asks, treading in place near the middle of the pool, water dripping onto his face.

"Not a chance," I say, my stockings reaching the edge of the concrete as the breeze blows my hair across my face. I tuck the rogue strands behind my ear and crouch.

Kade swims a little closer. "So you're just going to watch?"

"Like you've been watching me this whole time?" I challenge, sitting cross-legged, the dark blue fabric of my dress gathering in my lap.

He smirks. "I could pull you in here faster than you could blink."

My eyes narrow, and I freeze. "I'll kill you."

"Hmm," he hums, wading closer, "you've said that once before."

I nod. "And I meant it both times."

He tilts his head. "Now why would you want to do that

when we have so much fun?" He grips the ledge of the pool on either side of me, and my breath gets lodged in my throat.

"I'm not getting in the pool, Kade." There's an edge in my tone. *Don't you dare*, it warns.

He licks the water from his lips, and they curl into a slow grin. "Do you trust me?"

"Absolutely not," I say without missing a beat.

His grin widens as he stands, the pool shallow enough here that his upper half is above water. He wraps his hands around my ankles, murmuring, "You're a smart girl, Calla."

I bite into my bottom lip, my eyes dropping to where his fingers are warming my skin through my stockings. "What are you...? My stockings—"

"Will dry," he says, uncrossing my ankles and pulling my legs over the ledge. Before I can make a sound, they're submerged in the surprisingly warm water almost to my knees. His hands slide up my thighs, pushing my dress up to my waist.

I watch with bated breath, unable to move as the breeze in the air reaches the delicate skin between my legs, protected by nothing but the thin mesh of my stockings.

Kade snares my gaze, his fingers dancing across the inside of my thighs, higher and higher, until his thumb brushes my folds, and I suck in a sharp breath.

I can't believe this is the second time in two days he's touched me like this—or that I haven't stopped him.

He traces the line of my slit through the stockings, quickening my pulse at the promise of so much more in his eyes.

"What are you going to do?" I ask breathlessly, a flush creeping across my chest as my face floods with warmth. My eyes scan the yard quickly, but we're not close enough to any other house for a neighbor to see. But I'm still worried about getting caught.

"You wanted a distraction." His thumb brushes back and

forth, making it difficult for me to focus on his words. "That's why you're out here, avoiding the others with your nose in a textbook."

"I..." My voice trails off when his thumb circles my clit. Fuck, it feels so good.

"Let me distract you."

My head is spinning, hazy with lust and racing with panic. They're battling it out when I meet his gaze and the world narrows on this moment. I feel centered, yet in control of my body, so I know he's not messing with my mind.

I swallow past the dryness in my throat, and the moment I nod, he tears a gaping hole in my stockings. I gasp as the cool air assaults my bare thighs and the warmth between them. "I liked those," I mumble.

Kade peers up at me through thick lashes, only made darker by the water clung in them. "There are about a hundred identical pairs in your closet."

I nod absently, because he's no longer looking at my face. His gaze is locked between my legs as he grips my thighs and spreads them open at an agonizingly slow pace. He's teasing me, and I'm already vibrating with need. I hate my body for betraying me so quickly, but when Kade lowers his face and presses his mouth against the inside of my thigh, those bitter thoughts scatter. His tongue swirls expertly against my skin, a promise of what's to come, and I lift my hand to his head, running my fingers through his wet hair as my head tips back and he gets closer to my core. The sun is peeking through the trees, warming my face, and my lips part in a silent gasp at the first swipe of his tongue along my slit. I'm spread wide open for him and it has my heart pounding almost painfully in my chest. He takes his time, each pass of his tongue lazy yet practiced. I can't get enough. My breathing quickens and my hips jerk off the concrete.

Kade pauses, glancing up at me. "Keep still," he orders in a deep voice.

I catch my bottom lip between my teeth, nodding.

He returns his attention to my pussy and continues his slow torture of winding me up until I'm biting my tongue so hard to keep from moaning I'm afraid I'll slice right through it any second.

His tongue swirls around my clit before his lips close around it and he starts sucking.

I see fucking stars.

Moaning loud, I grip the back of his head, holding him there or just holding on for dear life, I'm not even sure. I don't give a shit at this point, so long as he keeps going. "Kade," I breathe his name, my voice trembling with pleasure, and he presses his tongue flat against my clit. Without warning, he plunges two fingers inside me, and I cry out, fisting his hair. It only spurs him on, and now he's sucking hard and pulsing his fingers deep in my pussy, curling them in the most delicious way.

My other hand flexes against the concrete behind me, and when my hips lift, Kade hums against my clit. He pauses his thrusts but holds his fingers in me, which has me trying to move against him in an attempt to keep the friction building. "If I have to hold you down, that pretty little dress of yours is going to get wet." He nips the skin above my clit, and I jump in response, shivering at the warning in his voice.

I have nothing intelligent to offer, so I keep my mouth shut and continue circling my hips, urging him to move his fingers again.

"Wanton little thing, you are," he purrs, kissing my pussy softly before his fingers finally start thrusting again. He moves them slowly, pulling almost all the way out before pushing into me again and again.

My chest rises and falls fast, and I can't catch my breath.

Kade takes me even higher, sucking hard on my clit as his fingers hit that sweet spot inside over and over, hard and fast. I race toward the edge and fall right over, crying out my release as I come around his fingers. He laps at the over-sensitive skin as I ride the aftershocks of my orgasm and catch my breath.

"Fucking hell," I mumble almost incoherently and pull my hand out of his hair, pressing it against my pounding chest.

"I'll take that as a compliment." His voice is laced with arrogance, but I'm so doped up with pleasure, I couldn't care less. I've had boyfriends go down on me in the past, but no one as skilled as Kade. He can be smug all he wants, I'm the one who benefited from it.

I inch back from the edge of the pool and pull what's left of my stockings off, dropping them in a sopping pile of material next to me.

Kade chuckles, ducking under the water for a brief moment before coming back up and running his hand through his hair. It looks good slicked back, showing off the sharp angles of his cheekbones and jaw—and I am definitely staring.

I turn my gaze away, looking toward the house, and freeze when I see Gabriel standing in the window. I whip back around to look at Kade. "How long has he been standing there?"

Kade arches a brow and looks past me. He smirks when his eyes land on Gabriel. "Hmm, from the look on his face, I'd say long enough."

"What does that mean?" I ask, my voice pitching higher.

He licks his lips, eyes on me again. "He's jealous."

"Jealous," I echo, shaking my head. *Gabriel wants me too?*

Kade must see something in my expression, because he nods. "Don't look so shocked, Calla," he says in a teasing tone, but I'm already scrambling up and grabbing my things.

I hurry inside, my jaw clenched tight as I pass Gabriel and practically throw his jacket at him.

He grabs my wrist and pulls me around to face him. "Angel—"

"Let go of me." I attempt to free myself instantly, but he holds me easily.

With no effort, he slides two fingers under my chin and forces me to meet his gaze. "Why are you running from me?"

I blink at him, because I figured it was pretty obvious. "I don't... I didn't know you were standing there. If I had—"

"You wouldn't have let Kade devour you?" Those silver irises flick across my face, waiting for an answer.

"No," I force out, my cheeks flaming, and I don't know if that's true.

"You have no reason to be embarrassed." His low voice is stern but gentle. "So don't be."

"Great, I'm cured," I say under my breath, tugging my arm back, and his lip curls into a smile as he frees me from his grasp.

I don't stick around after that. Retreating to the bedroom my things are in, I close the door and change out of the dress that's still damp near the hemline. I drape it over the tub for now, not sure I want to go searching for the laundry room, and put on my favorite maroon Georgetown hoodie and black yoga pants. I'm not here to impress these assholes.

I grab my book bag and rummage through it for my phone, which is probably dead by now. I owe Brighton a lot more than a text, but that's really all I can offer her at this point. When I can't find my phone, I huff out a sigh. *Did I leave it at the hotel?* No, I remember slipping it into my bag. Anger simmers in me. They definitely took it.

I drop my bag on the end of the bed and walk out of the room, heading directly for Atlas.

After coming up empty on the second floor, I venture up

to the third, peeking in a couple of plain, undecorated bedrooms that look as if they could be hotel rooms, before finding a room with double frosted glass doors at the end of the hall. My bare feet are cold against the hard marble floor, and I walk into the room without knocking.

The room is full of windows—not shocking at this point. The amount of natural light in this place has to be some sort of vampire joke, especially considering they built the house. I barely register the rest of the tidy room before my eyes land on Atlas, standing behind a raised black desk, typing on a laptop.

He doesn't glance up from his screen until I'm standing right in front of it. "What?" he asks, his voice distant; I've interrupted something.

"I want my phone." I manage a level tone, but my back is rigid. "My friends are going to wonder why I'm not responding to messages. That's not me." My mind immediately goes to Brighton. She's probably freaking out, wondering what the hell happened to me last night.

"The friend who booked your suite at the Four Seasons?" he inquires.

I cross my arms. "I don't see why that matters." No way I'm going to let them near Brighton. "You can't expect to keep me locked up in here with zero communication with the outside world." My tone sharpens with each word. "Give me my fucking phone."

Atlas moves with speed my eyes can't track, and he's in front of me, glaring hard. "You are in no position to demand anything."

My eyes narrow as his breath stirs the hair at my temple. The faint scent of citrus tickles my nose, as if he'd just eaten an orange before I stormed in.

"I am not a dog," I snap, jabbing at his chest. "I will not sit and stay and do whatever just because you wish it."

His expression darkens, and he grips my hip, pushing me back into the desk. My breath halts at the flash of his fangs. "Shall we test that?"

A muscle ticks in my jaw, and I gnash my teeth together. "Sure, go ahead and glamour me to be your little puppet, because it's the only way I'll sit quietly." My tone is confident, but the truth is, I'm terrified he'll do it.

There's a low rumble in his chest, a growl. His eyes narrow on me, and I grip the desk to do something with my hands. "You are far more stubborn than I expected," he murmurs.

I blink at his admission. "What the hell *did* you expect?" I ask, incredulous. "I'm being held against my will because of something I had absolutely nothing to do with. You lot won't tell me a single thing about what's going to happen, and I'm just expected to sit by and be cool with it? Fuck that."

Atlas leans in until we're practically nose-to-nose and says, "You'd better get cool with it, Calla, and fast."

My hand brushes against something cold and metal, and before I know what's happening, I wrap my fingers around it and ram my arm forward with all the strength I've built over years of weight training.

*Holy shit. I just stabbed him.*

I pull my hand back in a flash, but the end of what appears to be a letter opener sticks out of his stomach.

Atlas glances down for a moment, then looks at me, his mouth set in a tight line. He slowly removes the blade, which is dripping blood on the wood floor at our feet. He doesn't seem to care and drops the letter opener on the desk before lifting his shirt to reveal the wound is sealing itself.

"That wasn't very nice." His voice is low, hard.

My mouth is dry as I back away. I make it a couple of steps before my back collides with a solid wall of muscle, and I whip around to find Lex smirking at me.

"You can't kill us," he says, nodding toward Atlas. "Not easily anyway, and you're wasting your energy trying."

"What would you suggest I do instead?" I snap back and instantly regret it when he arches a brow at me, as if I should know what his response would be.

I shake my head. "I want to know what the hell is going on around here. Why did you take me just to keep me in the dark? What's in this for you?"

Gabriel chooses that moment to slip into the room, glancing between the three of us, his gaze not missing a single detail—including the blood on the floor and desk. His eyes land on me, and he frowns. "You should be careful with your words, angel. Don't ask questions you're not ready to hear the answers to."

Despite the kindness he's shown me, I scowl at him. "What the fuck is that supposed to mean?"

"You want to know why we took you?" Lex says, almost sneering at me. "We were going to kill you. Your entire family, actually—what's left of it. We don't do loose ends."

The blood drains from my face as the world tilts around me. Death by vampire is how I figured I'd go for as long as I've known of their existence, but to hear my deepest fears confirmed out loud makes me want to vomit.

"We still might," he adds with a wink, "if you choose to continue misbehaving."

My stomach clenches as panic erupts in my chest. I want to leave, to put as much space between me and them as geographically possible, but Gabriel and Lex are blocking my path to the door, my escape route. Behind that thick wall of fear, though, is a burst of excitement. These guys want me— either to kill or fuck—and so long as the latter desire outweighs the former, I get to remain alive. And if I'm being honest, the danger—the knowledge that they can take anything from me at any moment—is wickedly arousing, and I hate myself for wanting it.

Lex steps closer, his fangs descending from his gums. "Why do I think you're going to continue testing us?" He cocks his head to the side while Gabriel leans in the doorway, observing the exchange. "You're curious," he says, again moving closer. He's a mere foot away now, and I can't stop staring at his fangs. "You can't stop thinking about what we're going to do with you."

I open my mouth to shoot that down, but I can't make the words form on my lips.

"You want it as much as we do, don't you?" He reaches for my face, but something in me clicks on and I flinch back, then take off out of the room, brushing past Gabriel on my way through the door. He doesn't try to stop me this time.

Back in my room, I close the door and fall back against it, clutching my chest.

*What the hell am I doing?*

My heart beats hard and fast, and much lower, my center throbs. There's a part of me, no matter how small, that wants them. I crave the danger they offer, the fear that sparks deep inside when I test their limits. But will I survive when their control breaks?

## 6

I wonder if I can request a TV for my prison cell.

As I lay in the bed staring at the ceiling, I wish I could turn on *Scandal* and forget all about the vampires that own me, and instead focus on the crazy, twisted life of Olivia Pope.

A soft knock at the door turns my head toward it. I consider ignoring the sound, but they own the place. Whoever is on the other side could just as easily walk right in.

"Calla." Gabriel's voice is muffled through the door. "Can I come in?"

I purse my lips. He's asking permission? "Yeah," I finally say, and the door opens a moment later.

Gabriel walks in and closes the door behind him. "You doing okay?" he asks, approaching the bed.

I sit up, shrugging. "Sure."

He stares at me knowingly.

"Why are you so nice to me?" I ask in a low voice, pulling the black fleece throw blanket through my fingers. I keep my head down, focusing on the soft material in my hands.

Gabriel sits on the edge of the bed, keeping a comfortable enough distance. "Why shouldn't I be?" Of course, he had to go and turn the question back on me.

I look up at him. "Uh, maybe because you're holding me hostage?" I offer wryly. "Seriously, though. You're making it very difficult to hate you, which is necessary for me because—"

"Because you can't admit you might actually enjoy being here?"

"I... That doesn't matter. I *shouldn't* be here, and I sure as hell shouldn't enjoy it."

He nods thoughtfully. "Why not?"

I stare at him and am quickly reminded of how easy it is to get lost in his silver gaze, glamour or no. "Are you kidding?"

"You don't *want* to want it, that doesn't mean you shouldn't."

I arch a brow, and my stomach knots. This conversation is very quickly going off the rails into *what the fuck* town. "You're really going to sit there and try to talk me into being totally okay with being, what, a sex slave to four vampires? A human juice box for all of you?"

His lips twitch. "I enjoy your humor. I recognize it's a defense mechanism, but enjoy it nonetheless." He pats my leg when I blow out a breath. "Give it a chance."

"'It.' Being a captive to a house of vampires."

He nods. "The sooner you accept it, the better it will be for you, angel. You have my word."

I roll my bottom lip between my teeth, battling with the voice of reason in my head, which is screaming at me to keep fighting. But at this moment, with Gabriel looking at me like I'm the only person on the planet, I lose the strength to deny my desires. A little distraction might do me some good, anyway.

"Calla—"

"I want you to kiss me," I whisper, looking up at him as my heart rate kicks up.

He shifts closer until we're a breath apart. His hand cups the side of my face, and I lean into his touch. I feel safe with Gabriel, though I can't for the life of me decipher why. I'm also not going to question it. Instead, I bring my mouth to his and close my eyes as our lips brush. Slow and soft. Gabriel is gentle with me, as if I'm moments away from shattering apart. It's… sweet.

Gabriel slides his arm around my back and pulls me forward until I'm pressed against him. My arms drape over his shoulders as he tips my head back, deepening the kiss. When his tongue darts out, my lips part to let him in. He makes a sound at the back of his throat, and the muscles in his arm tense around my back. Without warning, one of his fangs slices into my lip.

I pull back in a flash, and a drop of warmth rolls down my chin. I lick it away quickly, but Gabriel's eyes are locked on my mouth. My heart hammers in my chest as I slowly reach up and touch his lips with my finger. He opens his mouth enough for me to see his razor-sharp teeth, and I poke his fang with my finger, gasping softly when it breaks the skin and a bright red bead of blood appears. I stick my finger in my mouth and suck gently, watching as Gabriel's jaw locks.

I lean in again, hesitantly pressing my mouth against his. When he kisses me back, I know the exact moment when he tastes my blood. His entire body stiffens, and he inhales sharply through his nose. He sucks my bottom lip into his mouth, trying to taste more, but I'm quickly made aware it isn't enough when he pulls back and stares at me with liquid silver eyes.

"You want to bite me." My voice trembles.

His eyes dance across my face as if to gauge my reaction it

that. My belly swirls with nerves and excitement. I'm scared to bare myself to him, but tempted by the throbbing between my legs.

"Calla," he murmurs, gripping my hip with one hand and sliding the other up my arm to cup the side of my face.

"Will it hurt?" I ask softly.

When he smiles, the tips of his fangs show, making my pulse jump. "It can, but not like this."

I frown, swallowing hard. "What do you mean?"

"When a human offers themselves to a vampire, the bite can be pleasurable—euphoric even. Vampires can also glamour humans to feel that way if the vampire chooses. Otherwise, if the human is being forced, the pain can be excruciating."

I nod absently, a shiver running down my spine at the thought.

"I would never force you to do anything you don't want to do," he says in a hushed voice, his thumb grazing my cheek. And I might be the most naive person on the planet, but I believe him.

Gabriel presses his lips against my forehead in a gentle kiss, and my eyes close. Despite my racing heart, I force my muscle to relax and tilt my head to the side. Gabriel leans in, moving the hair away from my neck.

I expect him to hesitate, to ease into it. Instead, there's a flash of sharp pain that steals my breath—a brutal reminder that Gabriel is a vampire, a monster, and I have absolutely no power here—and then warmth floods through me. The pain is over in a matter of seconds, replaced with sensations I never could have imagined. The pull of his mouth at my throat has me throbbing in seconds as I lean into him, gripping the front of his shirt as he drinks deeply.

Every nerve ending in my body flares to life. My skin tingles and warms, and I feel as if I'm floating on a cloud. It's suddenly very difficult to remember why I don't want to be here, and I press my lips together to keep from moaning out loud.

Gabriel pulls back slowly, lapping at my neck for a few moments before kissing my cheek. Before either of us can speak, the door opens and Lex slips inside, closing it behind him. His eyes shift between us, and when he opens his mouth, his fangs glint in the light.

"I thought I smelled something sweet," he purrs, coming closer.

My head is light and hazy. "I taste sweet?" I ask without looking at Gabriel.

"You taste absolutely exquisite," he murmurs in my ear.

Lex crosses his arms, and my eyes go to his tattoos. "So that's what you kids are up to in here."

"Jealous?" I taunt, then clamp my mouth shut, because *where the hell did that come from?*

Lex smirks. "Fuck yes."

I inch back toward the headboard, and both vampires watch my every movement, making my heart race. I can clearly see which direction this is going in, and part of me wants it so much it's embarrassing. The other part, though, the rational one, isn't sure what to make of the situation. I feel safe with Gabriel, and as much of a wild card as Lex seems to me, the two of them together balance out my nerves. Of course the idea of that is beyond bizarre, but I've quickly come to the conclusion that my knowledge of vampires is detrimentally limited. I wasn't expecting the pull I feel toward them, and while I'm not sure if that has more to do with the blood oath or their vampiric lure, it's something I'm unable to ignore—or resist.

"Stay with us now, angel," Gabriel says in a soft tone, snagging my attention.

I take a deep breath and nod. "I'm here."

In the space of a heartbeat, Lex is at my side, leaning over the bed and tilting my face toward him with a gentle finger under my chin. "If you thought Kade was good, you have no idea what you're in for."

My eyes widen. "I think he'd disagree," I breathe. I don't have a chance to overanalyze this scenario, which is probably a good thing, because I am so out of my element it's not even funny.

"Hmm," Lex hums, leaning in until our noses touch, "allow me to prove him very wrong." In a flash, he grabs my hips and pulls me down so my head rests on the pile of pillows at the headboard. I wet my lips, pressing them together as he slides his hands down my thighs. He keeps his eyes locked on my face, making my cheeks flush, and Gabriel moves up the bed and leans in to kiss my neck. He nuzzles my skin with his nose, inhaling deeply.

Lex trails his fingers back up my legs and curls them around the waistband of my yoga pants. He flashes a wicked smirk in my direction before slowly dragging my pants down my thighs. His eyes flash with something dark when he realizes I'm not wearing panties, and my breath catches in my throat. He looks about two seconds away from devouring me whole, and I probably wouldn't mind it.

He tugs my pants off the rest of the way, tossing them behind him before dropping his lips to my left ankle. He moves achingly slow, peppering feather-light kisses against my skin every inch or so until he reaches my knee, and then he does the same thing on the other side.

I'm vibrating with anticipation, and a pulse of excitement bursts through me when Gabriel's fangs scrape my neck, not breaking the skin but tempting me with the promise of pleasure. He slides in behind me and pulls me against his chest, wrapping his warm arms around me.

I catch my bottom lip between my teeth, tilting my head

to the side just enough that I can still watch Lex as his tongue darts out to lick the inside of my thigh. Heat rises in my chest and pools in my belly when he lifts his gaze to mine for a brief moment before his face disappears between my legs.

My entire world narrows on the feel of his tongue against my pussy. I grip the sheets on either side of me, and Gabriel grabs my hands, entwining our fingers and squeezing gently. He sucks gently on my neck, teasing me to the point of insanity. I can't bring myself to ask him to bite me, though I'm not sure why.

Lex pulls back with a hooded gaze, looking between Gabriel and me. "Bite her," he says in a husky tone, and my stomach clenches with excitement. Vampires aren't mind readers—that I know of—so Lex must've seen something in my gaze that showed him exactly what I wanted.

Gabriel's fangs sink into the same spot in my throat as Lex spears me with his tongue. I cry out, holding Gabriel's hands in a death grip that he probably barely feels.

Lex leans back, pulling his tongue out. "Spread your legs wider," he orders, and I comply way too fast. Clearly, I've decided to throw inhibitions out the window tonight. This situation really doesn't leave room for them, anyway.

"Good girl," he praises, flicking my clit with his thumb as he dives back between my legs, thrusting harder and faster until my head spins and I'm gasping for air.

Between the sensations of Gabriel drinking from my neck and Lex devouring me with his mouth, I topple over the edge and shatter apart, my pussy walls clenching hard and my hips jerking off the bed. My moans fill the room, and I couldn't care less if the entire house hears my release.

Lex removes his tongue, circling my clit and making me jump as my chest heaves. Gabriel licks the wound on my neck until it stops bleeding, and my skin tingles in response.

"Fucking hell," I mutter under my breath. My heartbeat

pounds in my throat, and I'm so spent I can barely open my eyes.

"Don't worry," Lex says, patting my knee, "I won't tell Kade you enjoyed me better."

I try to scowl, but it comes out more like a purr, and my eyes won't even open now. "What does this mean?" I ask in a tired voice.

"What does what mean, angel?" Gabriel asks.

"You drinking from me," I whisper. It's probably something I should've asked *before* he bit me, but hindsight and all that.

"We're all already connected by blood, so this doesn't change anything."

Lex traces slow circles along my thigh. "Blood sharing on the other hand…"

I press my lips together and pry my eyes open to look at him. "Blood sharing?"

"If we drank from each other at the same time, it creates a sort of connection," Gabriel explains. "It's temporary and wears off after a few days, but can be very powerful the first time you experience it. You'd be able to sense me as much as I can sense you after drinking your blood. We would feel each other's emotions, and it would also draw us together in the sense that being apart would be unpleasant."

"Oh." The thought of drinking blood makes my stomach churn. I'm not squeamish by any means, but drinking blood? Hell to the no. And being connected to any one of these guys on that level seems like a very dangerous thing. The blood oath connection they have to me is invasive enough.

The corner of Lex's mouth kicks up. "It can also be very fun," he points out, shooting me yet another wink as he gets off the bed and heads toward the door.

I yawn. "Where are you going?"

Lex pauses in the doorway. "You're about to pass out, and

I've got some shit to do. Sweet dreams, Calla." He closes the door behind him as I yawn again and rest my head against Gabriel's chest. He hasn't made a move to leave, so I decide to get comfortable with him there.

He smooths a hand over my hair, and my breathing evens out. Before long, I drift off, vaguely registering a blanket being pulled over my bare legs. Sleep drags me under fast, and I don't fight it.

## 7

Sun streaks through the windows when I pry my eyes open for the first time in what feels like days. My muscles are tight, not painfully so, but certainly enough for me to notice.

*Shit. How long did I sleep?*

I dreamed of Gabriel and Lex, playing my body like an instrument they'd had an eternity of practice to master and making me explode with the most intense orgasm I've ever experienced. Not to mention, I never could have imagined what being bitten would feel like, but if it felt that good in my dreams, could it be that good in reality?

I sit up, stretching my legs out and yawning as I peek around the quiet space. My eyes land on my yoga pants in a pile on the floor, and I pause. "What the fu…" My voice trails off. *No. There's no way.* I lift a shaky hand to my neck, and when my fingers brush over two puncture marks, I suck in a sharp breath. I squeeze my eyes shut as last night's very real events come rushing back in a flash of fangs and pleasure.

I let Gabriel bite me. More than that, I *liked* it. Way too damn much.

And Lex...

"Oh my god," I whisper to the empty room, prying my eyes open again. I... I can't believe I allowed that to happen. Hell, that I asked for it. I wanted a distraction, and those guys sure knew how to deliver.

Reality crashes down on me like an emotional hangover, and I want nothing more than to pull the blankets over my face and pretend last night didn't happen.

I need to find a way out of this stupid arrangement—preferably before my traitorous body tricks me into wanting to stay.

I pull myself out of bed and get in the shower, turning the dial until the heat of the water fills the room with steam. I wash my hair, then cover it in a generous amount of conditioner, leaving it in while I lather my body with a rose-scented scrub, flinching when some of the soap gets in the bite mark on my neck. I tip my head back to rinse it, then finish showering quickly before shutting off the water and stepping out into the warm haze. My toes wiggle against the plush bathmat as I grab a white terrycloth robe and pull it on.

Standing in front of the steam-covered mirror, I wipe my hand across it and lean in to inspect the small holes in my neck. I poke at them gently. The skin is tender, but it doesn't look so bad. I figure attempting to cover it up with makeup will only amuse my new vampire roommates, so I elect to cover it with my hair instead. No need to put it on display. No doubt the entire house smelled my blood the moment Gabriel's fangs pierced my skin.

I shiver at the memory, biting my lip as heat pools low in my belly and my clit pulses. I scowl at myself. I need to get my shit together.

Walking through the bathroom into the ridiculously massive closet, I stop short, and my brows pull together.

Someone has filled the room with clothes. I pad across the marble floor, trailing my fingers along the muted, neutral colors. Everything is incredibly soft, and I bet stupid expensive.

*They essentially bought you,* a voice in the back of my mind says. *Might as well let them buy you some nice clothes.*

As much as I want to argue that, I can't stop myself from pulling a beige turtleneck sweater off one of the gold hangers. I purse my lips at it before setting it on the cushion-top ottoman in the middle of the room. *Too obvious.*

I settle on a black tank top with a heavy knit beige cardigan overtop and gray leggings. After scowling at the copious amounts of lingerie, I pick a matching black lace bra and panty set and get changed before combing my fingers through my hair and walking downstairs, my nerves as jittery as if I'd had several cups of coffee.

The guys are all here. Lex and Atlas are sitting on the couch in the living room with some news station on the TV built into the wall next to the door leading to the garage, Kade is in the kitchen making coffee, and Gabriel is sitting at the dining table reading something on a tablet.

I pause in the doorway of the hallway, glancing around the room at each of them. Gabriel meets my gaze first, setting the tablet on the table in front of him.

Taking a deep breath, I step into the room and clear my throat. "I have something to say," I announce.

Kade leans against the counter, wearing nothing but black joggers that sit dangerously low on his hips. His hair is damp and messy as if he haphazardly towel-dried it after a swim or shower. He takes a drink from his mug, while Lex turns down the volume on the TV and he and Atlas walk into the kitchen. Atlas is already dressed for the day in a black collared button-up and slacks, where Lex looks as if he's ready for a workout in a white muscle shirt that shows off his tattoos and gray sweatpants that leave little to the imagination in the groin area.

*Nope*, I scold myself. I have to focus.

"What is it?" Gabriel speaks up, remaining at the table, though I have his full attention. He's wearing a plain navy blue T-shirt, which has me assuming he isn't going to work today, and considering it's a Sunday, I suppose that makes sense.

I bite the inside of my cheek, panicking now that I have the opportunity to speak. Swallowing hard, I finally say, "My ancestors made a deal with the four of you a long time ago that decided the fate of my future before I was even born." I leave the bitterness out of my tone, though it lives on in me, because I'd just be talking in circles forever about how unfair it is that a bunch of men chose what would happen to me and I never had a say. There's no sense wasting my breath at this point.

I look from one vampire to the next until my gaze finally lands on Atlas. "I want to make a deal of my own."

Atlas tilts his head, regarding me curiously.

"What kind of deal?" Kade asks.

I keep my eyes on Atlas. "I won't try to kill you—again. I'll stay here," I swallow and force out, "willingly, for however long I'm obligated."

"In return for what exactly?" Gabriel asks.

"We could easily make you do that regardless," Lex adds with a quick wink.

I ignore him despite the fact that he's right. "I want to finish school. It's important to me. From there, I'm not sure, but I would like the option to renegotiate when the time comes."

"Renegotiate," Kade echoes, and I look at him this time before he continues, "what makes you think you have any leg to stand on to negotiate in the first place?"

My eyes narrow slightly. "The fact you haven't killed me."

"It's been two days," he says, a dangerous glint in his silver eyes. "Don't rush me."

I cross my arms over my chest. "You won't scare me into compliance, and I can't imagine a glamoured human would make for much entertainment, so don't bother with that threat again." I don't direct the second half to Kade, but to all of them.

Gabriel finishes off the glass of orange juice that had been sitting in front of him, then sighs.

Before he can speak, I say, "I'm not asking for much. If anything, my continuing to go to school would be good for you guys. You wouldn't have to figure out how to explain why I'm suddenly nowhere to be found after paying thousands of dollars to attend classes."

Kade and Atlas exchange a glance, and the latter vampire shrugs. Annoyance flickers through me, but I shove it down. I can't let my attitude or sharp tongue get in the way of potential partial freedom.

"Fine," Atlas says at last, and my heart skips a beat. I had been prepared to beg, though I'm relieved it didn't come to that. "There will be rules," he adds. "You will remain living here while you complete your degree."

"What about my apartment?"

"I've terminated your lease," Lex says.

I turn to him, arching a brow. "What are you talking about? How?"

"Lex owns the building you were living in," Kade chimes in.

My eyes go wide. "You what?" I demand.

Lex shrugs. "I have many investment properties. It's good business."

"I don't…" I shake my head. "This just keeps getting more fucked up." I rake my fingers through my hair, and Kade's eyes go to my neck. I quickly remember the marks there and pull my hair around to cover them again, but it's too late. He's seen them. His eyes meet mine and glimmer with heat. It makes me want to back away, but I keep my feet planted in place, counting on him not chomping down on my neck in the middle of the kitchen, though he looks as though he would like to do nothing more.

"You're lucky we are granting you any freedom," Kade points out, flicking his tongue along his bottom lip, and my breath catches at the glint of his fangs in the light from the window across the room.

I keep my mouth shut that time.

"I'll have the rest of your things brought here over the next few days." Lex's words are final. There's no negotiating this term, it seems.

I nod reluctantly. "Any other rules?" I'm unable to hide the agitation in my voice now, and Kade's expression darkens, though the smirk on his lips contradicts it.

"You will be held under glamour to come and go from your classes as we direct."

My mouth goes dry. The thought of being glamoured close to every day makes my stomach flip unpleasantly. "Why?" I force out. "You don't trust me not to run again?"

"Exactly," Lex says, looking rather amused at the thought. "I, for one, wouldn't mind chasing you, but the others aren't always in the mood to play."

My stomach is a pit of anxiety, but I say, "Fine. If that's what it takes to get out of this house for a few hours, I'll do it."

"You won't notice the glamour is in place unless you try to disobey it," Gabriel says, getting up from the table and carrying his empty glass to the sink, then leans against the counter. He's trying to make me feel better about the idea of them controlling me, I think, but it doesn't help the weight pushing down on my chest.

"Okay," I say in a low voice. "I'm assuming the lot of you already have my class schedule?"

Atlas inclines his head in a subtle nod. It doesn't surprise me at this point. It's just another reminder of how little control I've always had over my own life. Perhaps one day I'll be able to come to terms with it more easily, but for now, I'm reserved to wallow in it.

Kade leaves the room and returns in under a minute. He stops in front of me and holds his hand out. I glance down and find a shiny new phone in his palm. Arching a brow, I gingerly take it from him.

"Our numbers are programmed into it already," Lex says.

"So are your parents'," Gabriel adds.

I look up and frown at him. "I haven't—" I stop myself. They don't need to know I've barely spoken to them in months. Maybe I should tell them Atlas, Kade, Lex, and Gabriel found me, but it's pointless. We both knew it was coming and that there was nothing we—or anyone else—could have done to stop it. Telling them I'm here now won't change a thing. "Thanks for the phone," I finally say, dropping it into the pocket of my cardigan and making a quick mental note to shoot Brighton a text to let her know I'm alive.

"You may want to block Kade's number," Lex says with a snicker. "Unless you enjoy unsolicited dick pics."

Kade's deep laugh fills the room. "Please. As if they would be unsolicited."

I roll my eyes, though I'm secretly grateful for the ease in tension. "Thanks for the heads up," I tell Lex, then slip around Kade to walk to the coffee machine. I tap my fingers against the counter, looking it over. The shitty coffee machine at my apartment had maybe three buttons. This one has a touch screen with so many options it's making me nervous I'll break the damn thing trying to make a simple cup of coffee.

"Can I make you something?" Gabriel leans against the counter, watching me.

I shake my head. "I should probably figure out how to use it, considering I'm going to be here for the foreseeable future."

His responding smile makes his eyes sparkle, and something tugs at my chest. I shove the sensation away, doing my best to ignore it as he reaches into the cupboard above the machine and pulls down a mug, holding it out to me.

I take it, murmuring a soft "thanks" as I set it under the machine's spout. After a few failed attempts at navigating the system under Gabriel's silent supervision, I finally figure it out, and the aroma of freshly brewed coffee fills the kitchen, making me sigh happily.

My future may be bleak, but at least there's coffee.

## 8

I've never been so happy for a Monday morning in my entire life.

I get up and into a steaming hot shower without snoozing my alarm. I stop in the closet and grab blindly, dressing in a pair of black high-waisted pants and a turquoise blouse. I tuck it into the pants and slide on a pair of plain black flats before grabbing my book bag and my phone off the charger on the nightstand.

The kitchen smells faintly of cologne and coffee but is empty when I walk in. A burst of hope lights in my chest that I might be able to slip out without having to—

"Good morning." Kade's voice in my ear makes me jump and spin around to find him smirking at me.

"Do you have to do that?" I grumble.

His eyes glimmer with amusement. "I enjoy the little noises you make when I sneak up on you."

I don't offer a response to that. Anything I could say would only encourage his annoying as fuck behavior, and I have to deal with it enough already. "Where are the others?" I ask instead.

Kade thrusts his fingers through his messy hair and shrugs. "I think Gabriel left for work. Lex is probably still sleeping, the lazy bastard, and Altas usually runs in the morning."

I nod. "I, uh, have brunch with Brighton at Kafe Leopold in a bit."

He tilts his head. "Really? I don't remember discussing that yesterday."

My molars grind, and I force my tone level when I say, "It's a weekly tradition we have. If I don't show up, she'll know something's wrong."

"Hmm," he hums, pursing his lips. "Fine." He reaches out and taps the tip of my nose before I can move away. "You better behave."

I roll my eyes. "Touché."

He catches my gaze, and the swirling silver traps me in place. "And once your class is finished this afternoon, you'll come back here."

Jaw clenched, I nod. "I'll come back here."

Kade blinks, severing the glamour, and grins. "Good. You don't want to be late. Gabriel mentioned something about making lasagna for dinner."

I arch a brow at him. "You know, for vampires, I've only seen you eat human food since I've been here."

"That's not entirely true, now is it?" He points at the side of my neck, and my cheeks flood with warmth.

"That's not what I meant." I pull my hair forward and make sure Gabriel's bite mark is covered, making a mental note to apply some concealer before I leave the house. "I guess I expected to find the fridge stocked with blood or something."

Kade presses his lips together against a smile. "We have a separate fridge for that. You're not our first human house guest, and, well, it would get awkward rather quickly if someone opened the fridge and found bags of blood."

"Yeah, fair point," I comment.

"You want a ride to brunch?" he asks.

"I'm good." Showing up to meet Brighton with Kade behind the wheel would not go over well, and I already have a ton of explaining to do. I adjust the bag on my shoulder and step around Kade. "Thanks though. I'll see you later." I walk out of the kitchen and slip into the bathroom on the main level to cover up the marks on my neck. My handiwork isn't flawless, but so long as I keep my hair down, it should be fine. I should probably also pick up a few fashionable scarves, because if I have to bet, this won't be the last time I need to cover my neck. I shiver at the thought, recalling the pleasure that came along with Gabriel's bite.

Kade has disappeared when I walk back out of the bathroom. I pull my phone out and order an Uber, walking to the front of the house to wait outside. The front door has a keypad that allows me to lock it, though I realize once I've done that I don't have the code to get back in.

The sun is shining today, making the cold wind somewhat tolerable. My car arrives a few minutes later, and the driver is quiet on the short ride to Kafe Leopold, which has been mine and Brighton's regular Monday brunch spot for over a year now. It's close to campus and the menu is great.

I thank the driver as I get out of the car, and the moment I shut the door, Brighton rushes over to me. Her usually calm and kind hazel eyes are wide and filled with barely restrained panic. Of course her golden eyeshadow and perfectly-winged eyeliner are flawless, as is the rest of her outfit, no doubt all brand name pieces I wouldn't dream of buying myself. I tend to feel a little plain standing next to my best friend sometimes, but that has absolutely nothing to do with her, really. She's been the most supportive person in my life since we met last year as freshmen. Looking at her, you might think she'd be stuck-up, with her Michael Kors tote bag and black tweed Chanel jacket, but she's the complete opposite. She'd do anything to help anybody without a second thought.

"What in the ever-loving fuck happened to you the other night?" Brighton demands, grabbing my arm and pulling me toward the building.

"Hello to you too," I say, trying to ease her panic before it morphs into full-blown hysteria.

She lets go of me as her eyes narrow. "Calla, I'm serious. You need to tell me what happened. Your *I'm fine, will explain everything soon* text from a new number was less than convincing." Her strawberry blonde hair blows across her face in the wind, and I immediately grab for my hair to make sure it's still covering my neck.

"I know," I tell her, glancing around as a few people pass us on the sidewalk. She deserves to know, I'm just not sure how or what exactly to tell her.

"I tried to get in contact with you all weekend," she continues. "I called and texted about a million times, went by your apartment, I even called your parents."

I freeze. "You what?"

She huffs out a breath. "I know you're not super close with them, I just—I was freaked, Calla. Anyway, your mom said she was going to get in contact with you. I was going to follow up with her today and call the police if she hadn't heard from you, but then I got your hella cryptic message."

My stomach sinks. If my mom tried texting or calling my phone after the guys took it... I never got her message. "She tried to contact me?"

Brighton nods. "After you called me Friday night, something felt off. So, yeah. I'm gonna need you to—"

"I'll pay you back for the suite at the Four Seasons," I rush to say. The last thing I want is for her to think I'm taking advantage of her seemingly endless supply of money.

Her brows raise, and she frowns. "Calla, I don't give a shit about the money. Let's just go inside and talk over some cherry scones and lattes. I need some sugar."

I catch my bottom lip between my teeth, glancing toward the busy restaurant. "I'm really not that hungry. Maybe we could just go for a walk along the waterfront before class?"

She hesitates, then nods. "Yeah, okay." Her tone is gentle, but concern underlies her words.

It's a short walk to the water, and I hug my jacket closer as the cold breeze coming off the Potomac River sends a shiver down my spine. The boardwalk along the river is almost empty, which is good considering what I'm going to tell Brighton... just as soon as I can come up with the words to explain the crazy that is my life. Being honest about what happened may not be the smartest thing, but Brighton is my closest friend, she's my family, and I trust her completely.

We pass a middle-aged man jogging with his golden retriever in the opposite direction before Brighton says, "Please start talking, Cal. You're freaking me out."

"Sorry," I mumble, "I just... This is going to sound insane. I'm very aware of that."

She stops walking, and her brows inch closer. "Oookay. So not making me feel any better."

I sigh heavily and glance around to make sure we're out of earshot to anyone who could potentially overhear me. "What I'm about to tell you needs to stay between us, okay? I mean it. You can't tell anyone, it's really important for you to know that." I wipe my palms against my thighs as my heart thumps in my chest.

"I swear," she promises in a firm tone, though her voice wavers slightly; she looks as scared as I feel. "Please just tell me."

"Friday night when I got home from the library, there were four guys in my apartment. They were there for me."

Her eyes go wide, and I hold up my hand when she opens her mouth to freak out at me.

I press my lips together for a moment. "I should back up and start at the beginning."

"The beginning," she echoes breathlessly, and I can see the panic in the rapid rise and fall of her chest.

"You know my family is from New York City, that I moved here from there to go to school. Well, a long time ago —like, way before I was born—my family was involved with some really shady stuff on Wall Street."

Brighton shakes her head. "What, like insider trading?" she asks, and before I can answer, she continues, "What does that have to do with you? Or these guys that you're saying broke into your apartment? I don't—"

"I'm getting there," I assure her, "but you need some background information or this is *really* going to sound crazy." It's going to regardless, but context might be something of a benefit when she attempts to rationalize what I'm telling her.

"Keep talking," she says, crossing her arms over her chest.

"The business my family was involved in was dangerous enough their lives were threatened by some very powerful people. These guys, they helped my great-great-grandfather out of the deal. In exchange, I..." I swallow to try and get rid of the dryness in my throat, but it barely makes a difference. "I was promised to them, as the first-born daughter of the Montgomery bloodline."

She blinks at me. Her hands fall to her sides, and she just keeps shaking her head as if she's trying to figure out what I said, as if I spoke in a different language and she's struggling to interpret it.

"Bri?" I ask softly, watching her face closely.

Her eyes meet mine. "Hang on. You said these guys made

a deal with your family before you were born and then they showed up at your apartment the other night?"

My stomach sinks. "Y-yes. They, um…" I lower my voice as dread coils in my chest, making it hard to breathe. "They're vampires."

Brighton chokes on a laugh. She keeps laughing until her eyes are glassy with tears, and I stand there and wait until the sound dies away. "Holy shit. You're being serious right now."

I nod. "Trust me, Bri, I wish I was kidding."

She doesn't meet my gaze, and her face has drained of color. "This isn't possible. Calla, what you're saying—"

"I know." I reach for her, grabbing her wrists, and she finally looks at me again. "I told you it would sound insane," I remind her.

She shakes her head again, and I can't imagine what's going through her thoughts right now. "I can't… This doesn't…" She presses her hand against her chest. "Son of a bitch, I can't breathe."

My eyes sting with tears, and I immediately wish I hadn't said anything, or that'd I'd come up with a better scenario I could give her. I'd be lying, but at least she wouldn't look absolutely petrified right now. I had years of knowing about the existence of vampires before they showed up in my life. I'm dropping this all in Brighton's lap without any warning. Her response is completely warranted. I just wish there was something I could do to make it easier on her.

"Look at me," I say firmly, tightening my grip on her wrists until she does. "I'm so sorry. You shouldn't have to know this, but I… I needed my best friend."

She blinks quickly, as if she's trying to fight back tears. "Calla, I don't know what to do with this." Her chin quivers, and she whispers, "Vampires aren't real." It sounds as if she's trying to convince herself, and it makes me feel even worse.

I bite my lip to keep it from trembling. "They are," I tell

her, wishing more than anything in the world that I was lying. "I don't know how populated the world is, but I know at least four of them."

When she blinks, a tear rolls down her cheek, but she makes no move to pull her hands back and wipe it away. She swallows hard. "W-why is this happening?"

"I'm so sorry," I repeat, because what else is there to say at this point?

Her lips turn down. "It doesn't make any sense," she says in a low voice. "Why... I mean how did this happen?"

I already told her why and how it happened, but I tell her again. I wouldn't be surprised if I triggered a shock response in her, so having to repeat myself is the least I can do, even though saying the words again only tightens the knot in my stomach.

She sniffles, straightening as her fear seems to shift toward anger. "They can't do this to you. We have to tell someone! I can talk to my grandfather. He's in with a lot of the high-level security guards in the city." She twists her wrist in my grasp and grabs ahold of me. "People can't own other people, Calla."

My temples ache with tension and bitterness fills my next words. "These aren't people."

"Ouch. Now that's not a very kind thing to say about someone."

I go stiff as a board at the sound of Lex's voice behind me, and Brighton's eyes almost pop out of her face.

*Son of a bitch.*

I squeeze Brighton's wrists until her terror-filled eyes flick back to me, and then I mouth one word: *run*. I let go of her and turn to face Lex, expecting to find a pissed-off vampire glaring at me.

Instead, he grins, and his voice is almost teasing when he says, "You're in big trouble."

A muscle ticks in my jaw as a dangerous mix of fear and anger flares in me. "I—" My voice cuts off at the sound of a scared gasp, and I whirl around to find Brighton made it about ten feet away before Kade blocked her path. *Where the fuck did he come from?*

Kade wraps his hands around Brighton's shoulders, snaring her gaze, and panic bursts like a firecracker in my chest.

"Don't you dare," I snarl at him, stepping toward them, but Lex snakes an arm around my waist and hauls me back. I whip my head around to make sure no one is paying attention, but there are even fewer people around and none close enough to see what's happening.

"Chill out, Calla," he says in my ear.

I slam my elbow back, trying to catch him in the stomach, but it does nothing. "Let me go," I demand through my teeth, all the while watching Kade speak softly to my best friend, her hazel eyes glazed over as he glamours her. "Kade, stop!" I pull against Lex's grip, but all it does is make my stomach hurt.

He ignores me and continues talking to Brighton. She nods along, and when she smiles, my posture goes rigid. I stop fighting. This was a huge mistake. I shouldn't have told her out in the open, I should have—

Kade turns his face toward me, and Brighton's gaze follows. He's still speaking to her, though I can't make out his words, and she's still nodding. Finally, he lets go of her shoulders, and she turns to walk in the opposite direction. Doesn't say a word to me, just keeps walking away without so much as a glance back.

Lex pulls his arm from around my waist as Kade approaches, and I stalk forward, closing the rest of the distance between us in a few angry strides.

"What the fuck was that?" I snap at him.

His silver eyes narrow. "That, Calla, was me correcting your mistake." His words are clipped. "And I believe the words you're looking for are *thank you*."

"How about *fuck you*?" I shoot back, clenching my hands into fists to stop myself from trying to punch his stupid face.

"Oh, we both know you don't have a problem with that," he taunts, his lips twisting into a smirk.

I ignore that, glancing around to make sure we're still out of earshot to the people around us. The foot traffic has picked up slightly, but no one is close enough to overhear when I say, "What did you say to her?"

Kade cocks his head to the side. "I told her you moved out of your apartment to live with a family friend. I also helped her remember her morning a bit differently than how it went down. You see, we don't particularly like when certain people know about our… lifestyle."

Lex snorts from behind me.

"Certain people? She's my best friend, Kade. You can't isolate me from the people I care about just because—"

"Yes, we can," he interrupts. "You know why? Because when you run your mouth to people that can use the knowledge of what we are in very dangerous ways—"

"Kade," Lex cuts in, and there's a warning in his voice.

"What the hell are you talking about?" I demand. "Brighton wouldn't tell anyone." Considering she said we should go to her grandfather for help, that's not entirely true, but if I asked, she would keep it secret.

"Not a risk we're willing to take," Kade says, his eyes trained on me.

"So, what? You followed me from the house?"

"Yep. Good thing, too. I guess we didn't think we had to tell you to keep our little arrangement to yourself."

I gape at him, incredulous. "Our *arrangement*." Shaking my

head, I continue, "You can't just… This isn't… I don't need a fucking babysitter."

"Clearly you do," Lex chimes in from behind me.

"Shut up," I snap over my shoulder before facing Kade again. "This is ridiculous, I—"

"Agreed," he says, cutting me off.

I shoot him a glare. "You have no idea how much I hate you right now."

Kade steps closer, filling my personal space with mint and the crisp scent of his cologne as he lowers his mouth to my ear. "And yet, I bet you'd still come all over my fingers. Again."

I open my mouth to fire back a venomous retort, but my breath catches in my throat. *Fucking bastard.*

Lex clears his throat. "All right, you two. Calla needs to get to class."

Kade moves away slowly, his gaze fixed on my mouth for a long moment before his eyes lift to mine, glimmering with a challenge. "We'd better get going then."

I finally find my voice and say, "We?"

"Uh-huh. You've made it perfectly clear you can't handle the freedom we so graciously offered you, so I'm going to accompany you to this afternoon's lecture."

"The hell you are," I snap angrily. The cool temperature and breeze coming off the water are no longer making me cold. The fire in my veins has made sweat dot my brow.

"Either Kade goes with you," Lex says, "or you're not going at all."

My gaze swings between the two vampires on either side of me. "You have got to be kidding me."

"Nope," Kade says, popping the 'p' with a shit-eating grin curling his lips. "And don't think I'll let you copy my notes."

It takes everything in me not to take a shot at pushing him into the river.

## 9

We walk in silence most of the way to campus until my stomach grumbles. I hadn't been hungry when I met up with Brighton, and as upset as I still am, I can't deny the pang of emptiness in my stomach.

Kade casts a sideways glance in my direction and arches a brow. "I heard that. We can stop at the Starbucks on M Street."

"I'm fine," I mutter, picking up my pace.

He catches my arm and pulls me back before pushing me against the side of a building, almost making me drop my book bag. "What you did was incredibly stupid."

My gaze whips around to make sure no one is looking, because this can't look very good, but we're on one of the quiet side streets; there's no one in sight. I scowl at him. "And what you did was incredibly invasive and wrong."

A muscle feathers along his jaw, and he shakes his head slowly, as if he's trying to control himself. "You have no fucking clue, Calla. None."

"And whose fault is that?" I fire back.

His silver eyes flare with anger, and he moves closer, pressing me into the cold brick. "You do something like that again, and you'll never see the outside of our house again. Understand?"

I glare at him. "You know, I thought you were the fun one and Atlas was the high-handed asshole." I tilt my chin up to meet his gaze and lower my voice. "I don't much like this look on you."

For a moment, he says nothing. His grip on my shoulders remains, and he just stares into my eyes. "No?" he finally whispers. "You prefer the look of me between your legs, don't you?"

My stomach clenches as his eyes drop to my mouth. "Honestly? Yeah." No sense in lying now. "And considering we can't do that here, I guess we better just go to class."

Still, he doesn't move. His gaze is locked on my lips, and it takes everything in me not to lick them, to beg him to kiss me. Because as pissed as I am about what happened with Brighton, I can't deny the way my body wants him. His exhale stirs the hair at my temple.

"Hmm." He steps back and waits for me to start walking before he falls into step beside me.

After a quick stop for food and caffeine, we get to campus and slip inside the lecture hall just as Professor Fischer opens her laptop at the front of the room. Some higher power must be looking out for me today, because there are still open seats in the corner of the room by the exit. I quickly take one of them and drag Kade down into the one next to me. The lights flick off, drowning the room in darkness as Fischer gestures to the projector screen behind her and starts talking about this week's reading.

I pull out my notebook and struggle with the little wooden table folded against the side of the theatre-style chair until it finally comes out, creaking as I secure it into place. Clicking my pen open, I do my best to pretend Kade isn't here and focus on the lecture.

It works... for about five minutes.

I can feel his eyes on me even in the dark, and his cologne is clouding my brain; he smells annoyingly good. The last thing I need is a distraction from my schoolwork, but evidently, my body didn't get the memo. I press my thighs together to sate the throbbing between them, and my cheeks burn when Kade chuckles under his breath.

*Fucking vampire senses.*

"Shut up," I hiss, keeping my eyes on the screen. The words could be in German for all I can tell at this point. My pulse is thunder beneath my skin, and it jackhammers when Kade reaches over and slides his hand up my leg. I suddenly wish I'd worn a dress today instead of high-waisted pants, because as much as I should push his hand away, I want nothing more than to press it against my core.

"Shh..." His lips are at my ear, and my eyes flutter shut.

"You can't," I whisper unevenly.

"I can," he says, and I can hear the smirk in his voice, "but you need to keep quiet."

I wet my lips, then press them together and open my legs a little. My heartbeat is in my throat, and I'm gripping the wooden arms of the chair as if I'm on a rollercoaster that's about to drop.

Kade flicks his tongue against the skin below my ear, and my breath catches as my eyes fly open. I force them to stay on the screen at the front of the room, though I haven't a clue what Fischer is talking about. Kade's fingers trail along the inside of my thigh, and I curse the universe for the existence of pants. He presses his lips against my neck, kissing and sucking gently, and when his hand cups me through my pants, the air halts in my lungs, and I clench my jaw to keep from making a sound.

"Good girl," he murmurs against my skin, pressing his thumb over my clit as his other fingers rub up and down and then in circles until my breathing quickens. My chest rises and falls quickly, and I desperately want his fingers inside me. He might be able to make me come this way, but it will feel so much better if he is actually *in* my pants.

"Kade," I whisper breathlessly, struggling to keep my eyes on the presentation.

His fingers stop moving and he says, "I know what you want."

I nod, finally looking at him to find his gaze filled with lust. A reflection of mine, I'm sure. "We should go." I can't remember the last time I left a lecture early, but I'm more than willing right now.

The corner of his mouth curls up, and he pulls his hand back, resting it in his lap and drumming his fingers against his thigh. "You wanted to go to school," he says, turning attention to the front of the room.

My mouth drops open, and I stare at him. "Are you serious right now?"

His smirk widens, but he doesn't look at me. "Shh, Calla. I'm trying to focus on the lecture."

I narrow my eyes and close my legs. "I hate you," I grumble, crossing my arms.

His soft chuckle is the only response I get.

※

After the longest lecture of my life, we stop at my apartment to pick up a few of my things.

I walk around the space and already miss it. I don't want to give it up. The coffee might be a million times better at the house, but this place… it was mine.

"Lex arranged for the movers to pick up the rest of your

things tomorrow," Kade says, leaning against the kitchen counter.

I nod absently, grabbing a few books off the coffee table and sliding them into my bag. I walk down the short hall and grab a few extra toiletries out of the bathroom, then stop in my bedroom. The twinkle lights on the wall my bed is up against are still on. I've never appreciated how small and cozy this space was until now. Now that I have to go back to a ridiculously fancy mansion full of vampires and play house.

I drop onto the end of the bed with a heavy sigh and stare at the wall. I covered it with pictures—mostly polaroids from Brighton's camera—from parties over the last couple of years. There's also a bunch of pictures from my travels before school started, and even a few from when I lived in New York City.

"Calla?" Kade's voice floats down the hall.

I get up and swallow hard, clearing my throat and blinking back the sting of tears that took me off guard. "Yeah, I'm almost ready." It's a total lie. I'm not ready to leave this behind.

Kade leans in the doorway, his eyes on me. A muscle ticks in his jaw as he frowns, and then he glances at the wall of photos. "You're quite the photographer," he comments, pushing away from the doorframe and walking into the room to get a closer look.

"Memories fade," I say, "photos are forever."

He plucks one from the wall, and I peek over his shoulder to see which one he took. It's a polaroid of me and Brighton at the Lincoln Memorial last summer. Her arm is draped over my shoulder, and she's kissing my cheek. We're both wearing these cheap, bright pink sunglasses we bought from a street vendor, and I'm grinning so hard it hurt my cheeks.

A pang of guilt weighs on my chest for what happened to

Brighton this morning. Even though she doesn't remember it, *I* know it happened.

I snatch the photo from him and slide it into my back pocket. "Let's just go," I mumble, heading for the hallway.

"I'm sorry."

His words make me stop. My brows knit as I turn around and look at him. His expression is hard to decipher, but it's free of the usual arrogance or amusement I'm used to seeing.

"For this morning. Your friend—"

"I really don't want to talk about this." Especially if he's going to be an asshole about it again.

"She can't know about us," he says in an even voice, though it's not filled with the same harsh tone as this morning. He almost sounds... sympathetic?

I nod without meeting his gaze. "She's all I have," I say, though I'm not sure why. He must know how important she is to me, considering all of them have been watching me for god knows how long. Still, I keep talking. "Growing up—well, in the years after my parents told me what was going to happen to me—I was careful about who I spent time with and who I let in. I decided very quickly that it wouldn't be fair to any friends I would possibly make if I just disappeared one day. I also didn't know what the four of you planned to do to anyone I was associated with, so I couldn't risk it. Brighton..." I trail off, shaking my head. "I tried to push her away. I was a total bitch, actually, when we met, because I liked her so much. Right from the start."

"For what it's worth, she seems like a good friend."

"She's one of the best people I've ever met. Her family, they have money and power, which in this city can be a dangerous combination, but you'd never know she had that kind of privilege. She's the kind of person who'd empty her wallet for someone struggling with homelessness and always make sure the people around her are okay." I can't help the smile that touches my lips. "She would go to war for me." I look at Kade. "And she'd sure as hell kick your ass if she knew the truth."

A ghost of a smile graces his lips. "I don't doubt that for a second." He steps toward me. "I'm not saying you can't be friends with her, Calla, you just can't tell her about the existence of vampires. People don't tend to take that very well."

"Yeah, I get it." There's an edge to my voice now. I get to keep my best friend, but I can't tell her about the biggest, most life-changing thing that will ever happen to me. No biggie, right?

"What does her family do?" he asks, glancing back toward the wall of photos.

I have to give him a little credit, I guess, that he's at least pretending to show genuine interest in my life—what it was before they waltzed into it a few days ago. "Um, I'm not totally sure. Honestly, I don't even think Brighton knows. Her parents own their own company and it has something to do with environmental stuff." I shrug. "I'm into social sciences, not bio and chem."

He chuckles. "Fair enough."

"Oh, and her grandfather is a senator." I'm pretty sure that's where most of their money comes from.

Kade turns back to me. "That's interesting."

"Sure, if you think politics is interesting."

"Don't you?" He tilts his head. "At least the kind on television, right?" His voice takes on a teasing lilt, and I scrunch up my nose. I'd told Gabriel about my love of *Scandal*, but evidently, Kade had overheard. That, or it was already something the lot of them knew about me, anyway.

"You're making fun of me."

The corner of his mouth kicks up. "Maybe a little."

"Don't knock it until you try it," I tell him.

He holds his hands up. "All right, all right. Maybe I'll give it a shot." He moves closer again. "Are you ready to go?"

I only nod, because I don't trust my voice not to crack. I don't want to leave, not again. Especially when I won't be back here again. The weight of that crashes down on me and panic surfaces in a rush, making my chest tight. I spin away and hurry out of the room, sucking in air and forcing it into my lungs as I try to focus on something, *anything* else.

Kade appears in front of me, and I jump back, gasping in surprise.

"Fucking vampire mojo," I grumble, still catching my breath as I meet his gaze.

"Look at me," he orders in that voice that latches on to the deepest parts of me and forces compliance. "You're okay. Take a deep breath and let it out slowly. The tightness in your chest will ease in a minute. Just keep breathing for me, okay?" He poses it as a question, though his glamour is making me do exactly as he says.

After a few deep breaths in and out, I'm feeling much better. My head is clear, and I don't feel the immediate need to run away from everything.

Kade steps in and holds my chin between his thumb and forefinger. "You are the most beautiful human I've laid eyes on, you know that?"

I lick my lips without thinking about it. "You don't have to keep trying to distract me," I murmur. "I'm fine."

He leans in until his lips are mere inches from mine. "I'm not," he says, his voice filled with sincerity. "I'm being selfish, actually."

"How so?"

He slides his fingers along my jaw to cup the side of my neck and tips my head back with his thumb under my chin so I'm looking into his eyes again. "Because all I've been thinking about since that boring as fuck lecture was how badly I want to devour you again."

My eyes widen slightly. Perhaps I should be used to his forwardness by now, but he still manages to catch me off guard when he says things like that. Things that make my heart race and my core clench with need.

He presses his lips against my temple and sighs. "Tell me no." His words make me shiver as he rests his other hand against my hip.

"Will you stop if I do?" I whisper, and the throbbing between my legs really hopes he doesn't.

There's a stretch of silence.

"No." His lips crash down on mine, and he grips my hips, hauling me against him. I close my eyes as he devours my mouth, and wrap my arms around his neck, clinging to him so tightly he can probably feel my heart pounding against my chest.

Kade kisses me until my head spins, until I'm breaking away to fill my lungs with air.

"We should go," I manage in between breaths, and put some distance between us. "I was supposed to go back to the house right after class, remember?"

He rolls his eyes, grinning. "And you are. We just took a little detour." He picks up the bag I dropped on the floor at some point—I hadn't even realized—and shoulders it.

We walk out of my apartment, and the sound of the door closing echoes down the hallway.

※

Back at the house, Lex and Gabriel are gone. I take my bag to my room and stop in the bathroom to freshen up before wandering around a bit. I've got some time to kill before dinner, and while I probably should review the online notes from today's lecture, it's the farthest thing from my mind.

I freeze in the hallway to Atlas's office when the sound of shouting reaches me. Frowning, I step closer once, twice, then once more until I'm standing outside the closed door. I can only make out every few words; it's as if he's walking—pacing more likely—closer to the door, but turning and marching away midway through his sentence.

"... By next week... what needs to be done... come down there myself and... I don't care how... Dante is not—"

Suddenly, I'm being pulled away from the door. A hand clamps over my mouth before I can scream, and when Kade's cologne wafts under my nose, I pull his hand away and whirl on him.

"What the fuck?" I hiss.

"Listening in on conversations you're not meant to be a part of is rude," he says, shaking his head at me as if I'm a child in need of scolding.

"Maybe if you weren't keeping me in the dark about, you know, *everything*, I wouldn't have to stoop to eavesdropping." I cross my arms over my chest and scowl at him. "Besides, I didn't mean to overhear anything. I was just looking for something to do to kill the time before the others get home for dinner."

Kade arches a brow at me. "I could give you several far more entertaining ideas than listening to Atlas blast someone."

"Oh, I'm sure," I remark dryly.

My head whips back toward the office door when Atlas shouts something, and a second later, the sound of shattering glass comes from behind the door.

"Ah, fuck," Kade mutters, stepping around me and knocking on the door before opening it slowly. "What's up, brother?"

Before he can say anything, I push past Kade and walk into the room.

Atlas stares at me for a moment before glancing toward Kade. "It's fine," he says in a low, gravelly voice.

"It didn't sound fine."

He moves in a blur and appears in front of me, so close the tops of his shoes touch mine. "And what exactly do you think you heard, Calla?" His voice is dark, venomous, and the flash of his fangs makes me stiffen.

I want nothing more than to move away, but I won't give him the satisfaction of making me back down. I also can't ignore that something about him, the darkness in him, draws me in. I want to test his limits. To see just how far I can push him before his control snaps. Clearly, my self-preservation hops on a train straight to crazy town when it comes to Atlas.

"She didn't hear anything," Kade says from behind me.

Atlas is still glowering at me. "Is that so?"

I hold my head high and my shoulders back. "You could tell me now," I offer.

Kade chuckles before exiting the room, the only indication that he left being the click of the door closing behind him.

Atlas purses his lips. "Oh, could I?" His tone is condescending. "I don't see that happening."

"And what exactly *do* you see happening?" I ask in a clipped voice, echoing his words.

He grabs my chin; it's not gentle the way Kade did earlier, and yet, my heart is still racing with anticipation. *What the fuck is wrong with me?*

"What's your angle?" I push, making no attempt to free myself from his grip. "There has to be some bigger reason you're keeping me here and alive. And I don't believe for a second that it's just to fuck and feed on me."

His eyes narrow ever so slightly, and he leans closer. His lips barely brush mine when he speaks. "Did it ever occur to you that maybe you should just be glad we're keeping you alive?"

I hold his gaze. "That's not good enough."

There's a flash of surprise in those bright silver eyes, but it's gone as quick as it came. He drops my chin and steps back. "Fine. You may come in handy with certain… business acquisitions."

I shake my head, clenching my hands into fists at my sides as annoyance fills me. "What the hell does that even mean?"

He shrugs. "Whatever I need it to."

I grit my teeth. "You are such an asshole."

Atlas says nothing to that. The second I trick myself into thinking I'm making a bit of progress here, I'm brutally reminded just how wrong I am when Atlas opens his mouth.

"Who is Dante?" I ask, watching him closely for any flicker of a response.

His jaw tightens before he exhales a dark, humorless laugh. "I thought you didn't hear anything."

I shrug and ask another question. "Is he a vampire?"

Atlas hesitates. His brows furrow as he seems to consider his answer. "Yes."

"You seemed angry on the phone. Why?"

He shakes his head. "Game over, Calla."

"Why?" I push.

"It's not your concern," he growls in my face.

I stand my ground. "I don't believe you. Otherwise, you wouldn't be so fucking uptight right now."

"I do not care what you believe. Now if you don't mind, I need to—"

"I do mind, actually," I cut him off in a sharp tone.

His lips press into a tight line, and he grabs my shoulder, holding me in an unbreakable grip as he drags me to the door. Ripping it open, he all but shoves me into the hallway and slams it in my face. It all happens too fast for me to have any reaction until we're separated by a thick pane of frosted glass.

I slam my fist against the door. "Asshole!" I storm back down the hallway, knowing I'm not going to get anywhere with Atlas. Gabriel, though, I might have a shot getting *something* out of. He seems to have a soft spot for me, and I am not above using that to get some information. Desperate times and all.

Walking back to my room, I close the door behind me. I pull out my phone and open a new message. I'm not sure what brings me to do it, but I start typing a message to my mom.

*It's Calla. I have a new number. And a new address—with roommates.*

I chew my bottom lip, reading the message over and over, debating on whether or not I want to send it. She knows they came for me based on what Brighton told me. With a sigh, I hit send and drop onto the end of my bed, staring at the ceiling until my eyes start staying closed longer with each blink. I'm dozing off when my ringtone blares, startling me awake and upright as I reach for my phone. I swipe across the screen three times before I manage to answer the call without checking the number.

"Hello?"

"Oh, my sweet Calla. It's so good to hear your voice."

"Hi, Mom." My voice cracks, and I pull the phone away from my ear and clear my throat before bringing it back and saying, "What's going on? Why are you calling me?"

She sniffles, and I can hear the pain in her voice when she says, "Your father is here, too."

My stomach drops and my grip on my phone tightens.

"Why are you calling?" I ask again, swallowing the lump that has gathered in my throat.

"I needed to hear your voice. After Brighton got in touch with us, I tried to reach you. I even looked into booking a flight there but... We're so sorry, Calla," Mom cries.

Dad clears his throat, and his voice is gruff. "We wish there was something we could do. If we could save you—"

"Please," I cut in, my chin wobbling as I fight back tears. "There isn't... You can't. You never could." This conversation is a perfectly painful example of why I've barely spoken to either of my parents since I graduated high school. As much as they can't handle the guilt over the deal my dad's family made, I can't deal with listening to them apologize. And it's only made worse by the fact my mom had no idea about the blood oath until it was too late. It was never her fault, and the guilt she carries makes me want to scream. It makes me want to hate my dad for keeping it from her, but even after all these years—even after being taken by vampires—I can't hate him. He's... he's my dad.

"How are you?" Mom asks in a quiet voice. "I mean, are you... Have they hurt you?"

I swallow the lump in my throat. "No. I'm okay, Mom."

She chokes on a sound of relief, and I squeeze my eyes shut.

"I have to go. I..." It takes me a few beats before I can speak again. "Please don't worry about me." I want to tell her not to call me again. That it's too hard to hear her voice—and dad's—but I can't bring myself to do it.

"I'm so sorry." She cries harder. "We love you so much, baby."

I shake my head, though they can't see it. "I love you." I end the call, and the phone slips out of my hand onto the bed. Tears slip down my cheeks, and the pressure in my chest from holding them back so long threatens to burst. I struggle to swallow the sob lodged in my throat. I choke on it, grabbing blindly for a pillow to muffle the sound. I cry into it, unable to hold back any longer. My shoulders shake and my head pounds, but that pain dulls in comparison to the agony of having my heart cleaved in two.

## 10

The smell of spices and tomatoes reaches me before I step into the kitchen a couple of hours later, where I find Gabriel cooking ground beef in a skillet on the stovetop.

"Calla," he greets in a low voice. It seems... off. Not kind or gentle like I'm used to. He must have gotten home a while ago, because he's wearing dark gray sweatpants and a black V-neck. There's no chance he wore that to work.

"Hey," I say, "I didn't know you were home."

He nods, smiling at me over his shoulder as he keeps stirring the meat, but his usually bright eyes are dull.

"Are you... um, okay?"

Gabriel sets the wooden spoon on the counter and turns to face me. "I'm glad to be home," he says in lieu of a real answer. "How was your day?"

I exhale heavily, leaning against the counter, and steal a mouthful of shredded cheese. I sprinkle it into my mouth and ask, "Did you talk to Kade?"

He arches a brow. "No?"

"My day was fine," I say, forcing a cheery tone.

He sighs, pinching the bridge of his nose. "What did Kade do?"

"Nothing." I wave him off. "Never mind. Tell me about your day."

He gives me a knowing look. "Let's both agree not to talk about our days and make dinner instead. Sound good?"

I nod, coming around the counter. "I talked to my parents," I blurt, then press my lips together. *Where did that come from?* I shouldn't have said anything. This is something I should be talking to Brighton about. If I *could* talk to her about it...

"You did?" Gabriel asks; I have his full attention. "What happened?"

I run my fingers through my hair to have something to do with my hands and watch the ground beef sizzling in the skillet. "Not much of anything. They asked how I was, and my mom got all emotional and apologized. As if any of this is her fault." I pause. "I wanted to tell them not to call again, but I couldn't do it."

He frowns. "Calla—"

"*What*, Gabriel?" My voice comes out harsher than I was expecting. I swallow past the lump in my throat. "Should I have told them everything was great and invited them to come visit?"

His gaze softens. "I'm sure your relationship with them is complicated."

"Yeah," I say without meeting his gaze. *Which is partially your fault*, I don't add, though part of me wants to.

Gabriel glances toward the counter where his phone is vibrating. "Excuse me. I need to take this." He picks it up and answers in a hushed voice. His expression darkens, and he looks at me for a fleeting moment before leaving the room.

So much for getting any information from Gabriel. I sigh to the empty room. I'll have to try after dinner.

Approaching the stovetop built into the island, I pick up the wooden spoon and start pushing around the meat, hoping Gabriel will return in enough time to finish cooking, because it is definitely not my forte.

"Something smells delicious."

I jump a little, turning my head to look over my shoulder, and see Lex walking into the room, grinning softly as he rakes his fingers through his white hair only for it to flop back across his forehead.

"I thought Gabriel was cooking," he comments, walking closer and leaning against the counter next to me.

"He was," I say. "Someone called him, and he left looking all weird and tense." I force a nonchalant shrug. "I have no idea what I'm doing, by the way. You should probably take over if you want this to be edible."

Lex presses his lips together against a smile and comes up behind me. His arm brushes my side as he reaches for the spoon and keeps stirring. His chest is against my back, but I don't move away.

"What did you do today?" I ask to fill the silence and to distract myself from wanting to lean back into Lex. He smells of citrus and spice, a perfect fall evening, and it makes me want to wrap myself in it—in *him*.

He switches the burner off and drops his hand to my hip. "Nothing exciting." His voice is low in my ear, his lips close enough his breath tickles the shell of my ear.

I shiver, fighting the urge to close my eyes. "Same here," I lie. That lecture was the most exciting one I've attended all semester.

"Oh yeah?" he asks, then presses his lips against the skin just below my ear. His tongue flicks out, and I hold my breath.

"Lex..." I whisper.

"I want to fuck you against the counter," he murmurs,

and my stomach clenches. "I'd lay you down on the marble and spread those lovely thighs of yours. I'd have you screaming so fast you wouldn't have a chance to be embarrassed that the entire house could hear you moan my name. Though I do enjoy that beautiful pink your cheeks go when you blush."

The heat in my belly spreads lower, making my core throb with desire. My pulse kicks up and it quickly becomes hard to swallow.

"What do you think?" he asks, nipping my earlobe. Without warning, he turns me around and presses me into the counter next to the stovetop. "There's that blush I enjoy," he says with a wink.

I bite my lip, my eyes flicking between his as I lift my hand to his chest, running my fingers upward slowly. His black sweater is soft to the touch; I have the fleeting idea to steal it for myself, though I have a feeling he'd remove it pretty easily if I asked right now. I inhale slowly, overwhelmed by his scent now that I'm facing him. I lean up on my tiptoes and brush my lips across his. "I have no idea what I'm doing." I repeat the words, though I'm no longer talking about cooking.

"You're doing just fine," he says in a low voice, kissing the corner of my mouth, coaxing me to keep going.

I thread my fingers together behind his neck and lean in until we're pressed against each other. I kiss him again, longer and deeper, my heart hammering in my chest. My eyes close as Lex deepens the kiss, his tongue darting out to tease my lips until they part to let him in. I gasp into his mouth when he presses his lower half into me and his erection finds the throbbing between my legs.

"Fuck," he growls against my lips, kissing me harder.

My head spins, and I feel light enough to float away. I grind against him, desperate to ease the ache at my core, but

I can't get him close enough to do much besides feed the friction there.

"Calla." There's a warning in his voice.

I ignore it. "Just… kiss me," I plead, gripping the hair at the back of his neck.

He tips my head back and seals his lips over mine once more. We move together as if we've known each other for years, completely in sync. And when his fangs extend and slice into my bottom lip, I don't pull away.

Lex makes a deep sound at the back of his throat and tightens his grip on me, holding on as if he's trying to control himself.

I should be afraid, but my head is so hazy with lust, the thought doesn't have a chance to manifest enough to invite fear in.

Our kisses become quicker, more frantic, until Lex finally rips his mouth away from mine.

I blink my eyes open as I'm catching my breath and find him licking my blood off his lips, his fangs still fully extended and stained in red.

*Holy fuck that was hot.*

I lick the rest of the blood from my lips, which tingle at the touch.

"Do you want to know what you taste like?" Lex asks, running his thumb along his bottom lip.

My heart falters, and I open my mouth to respond, but nothing comes out. "I…"

He grins. "Everyone tastes a little different. You… taste like the warmth of the sun on your face after a long, dark winter."

"That's poetic," I mutter, heat rising in my cheeks.

His eyes hold mine as he shrugs. "Ask Gabriel what you taste like to him next time."

I choke on a laugh. "Yeah, I'm not going to do that."

That earns me another grin. "You also taste a little like strawberries and coffee."

I blink at him. "Are you serious?"

He nods. "As a white ash stake to the heart."

I arch a brow, making a mental note of that. You know, just in case. "Plain old wood won't do it?"

Lex pauses, seeming to consider his next sentence before he says, "No. Has to be white ash. Lucky for us, it's pretty rare."

"Huh. And that's the only way to kill a vampire?"

"Subtle," he murmurs, tutting his tongue. "You think I'm going to stand here and tell you how to kill me"

I prop my hands on my hips. "Haven't you already?"

The corner of his mouth kicks up; he isn't concerned. "You're very sneaky. Distracting me with your lips and your blood—"

"Hey, *you* bit *me*," I remind him.

"Yeah, I did. After *you* kissed *me*," he shoots back in a teasing tone.

"Whatever," I grumble halfheartedly, but before I can say anything else, Gabriel returns, and I catch his gaze. "Everything okay?" I ask.

He nods, offering me a smile. "Just something at work. Nothing you need to be concerned about."

I press my lips together, nodding, though I'm not sure I fully believe him.

"Fire them," Lex says, leaning against the counter.

Gabriel arches a brow at him. "Helpful as always, Lex. Thank you very much."

"Anytime." He winks.

Gabriel finishes dinner while I pretty much try to stay out of the way and just watch.

An hour later, the five of us are sitting around the table eating the most delicious lasagna I've ever tasted. I stuff my face with carbs, savoring the garlic bread Gabriel made to go with the lasagna and hating myself for how much I'm enjoying it. I almost forgot for a moment what circumstances led me here. Almost.

I take a long drink of water, glancing around the table. The guys are mostly quiet. Kade is scrolling on his phone, and Gabriel is speaking softly to Atlas, who is nodding along. Before my gaze reaches Lex, I freeze at the feel of his fingers trailing up my leg. Shooting him a look, I press my lips together as my cheeks flush. *He isn't going to...*

Lex's fingers slide between my legs and rub slow, firm circles against my center, over my joggers.

My jaw clenches so hard I can't open my mouth. I bite my tongue to keep from making a sound and fight the urge to push against his fingers.

I clear my throat and suck in a breath, flushing hotly when Kade peers over at me. *Shit.*

"You good?" he asks, arching a brow.

"I… Yeah, I'm fine," I manage to say before dropping my gaze to my plate. It takes everything in me to pick up my fork and lift it to my mouth, as if Lex isn't teasing me under the table.

When he pulls his fingers away, my stomach drops, either from relief or disappointment, I'm not even sure at this point. And then he slips them past the waistband of my joggers, and I see red. His lips twist into a satisfied smirk when he realizes I'm not wearing any panties, and he wastes no time, parting my folds and slipping inside in seconds.

*Fuck. Me.*

I squeeze my thighs together, cursing silently and gripping my fork tighter.

"Calla?" Gabriel's voice cuts through the haze of pleasure, and my head snaps up to look at him.

"Huh? Sorry, pardon?" I mumble.

He watches me for a moment that seems to stretch into forever, while Lex continues stroking me. "Are you not enjoying it?" he asks, pointing to the barely eaten lasagna that I've been pushing around my plate.

"Oh, no I definitely… am enjoying it."

Lex snickers beside me, slipping his finger out and circling my clit.

I manage to shove his hand away without being too obvious about it and return my attention to my plate. "It's really good, Gabriel," I tell him with a smile. "You'll have to teach me how to cook, because I pretty much tap out after instant noodles or those frozen meals you cook in the microwave."

Kade sucks in a breath and laughs. "I think you've traumatized him."

"What?" I say, chewing my lip. "Sorry, I just… I'm not good at cooking."

Gabriel's expression is priceless—it's as if I've just insulted his ancestors or something.

I arch a brow at Gabriel. "You going to live?"

His lips finally curve into that smile I've come to be rather fond of. "I'm going to teach you, because this is simply unacceptable."

I smile a little, then lift a piece of lasagna to my mouth and chew. "Deal."

---

I'm cleaning up after dinner when Lex slides in behind me, circling his arm around my waist and tugging me back against him.

"Come with me," he says, his lips brushing the shell of my ear and making me squirm and turn in his grasp.

My eyes flick between his, which are glimmering with

what I can only describe as excitement, though there's underlying darkness in them too. I've come to realize that's just his normal look, though—a little wild. "Where?"

The corner of his mouth kicks up. "My favorite place."

I arch a brow. "Not really a helpful answer, Lex."

He leans in, lifting his other hand and using his pinky finger to move a few rogue pieces of hair away from my face. I hold my breath—and his gaze—until he says, "I have an appointment with my tattoo artist. I want you to come."

A burst of excitement flares in my belly, and I can't help the smile that forms on my lips. I'm more than happy to get out of this house for a while, and I've never been inside a tattoo parlor. "Yeah, okay."

Before I know what he's doing, he dips his face and kisses my cheek, then steps back. "Meet me in the garage in half an hour."

I retreat to my room and change into a warmer shirt, adding a denim jacket, and tug on my Doc Martens. After pulling a comb through my hair, I twist it into a messy bun on the top of my head and grab my phone from the table beside my bed on my way out of the room.

Lex is leaning against the wall beside the garage door when I walk into the living room, and there's a little bounce in my step as I approach, which he picks up on and grins.

"Remember what I said," Kade says from the couch, and I turn my head to look at him. I haven't even noticed him sprawled there on his phone. "If you're going to get my name in a heart, I want it to be atomically correct." He's talking to Lex, who rolls his eyes in response. Kade's gaze shifts to me. "And what's our girl getting?"

*Our girl.*

Those words make my pulse jump, and I shake my head. "I'm just going to watch."

His eyes sparkle with mischief. "Watching can be fun."

It's my turn to roll my eyes as I turn back to Lex, and he opens the garage door, gesturing for me to walk ahead of him. I step into the concrete room and peer around at the collection of high-end cars.

"Pick one," Lex says, pausing at the wall with a board of key fobs.

I purse my lips, trailing my gaze over the selection before pointing to the sleek black Tesla.

"Good choice." He grabs a key, and I follow him to the car. He opens the passenger side, and I slide in. Moving too fast for my eyes to track, he gets behind the wheel and starts the engine. The car runs silently as we drive out of the garage, the door opening then closing behind us.

It's dark and unseasonably chilly outside as we drive toward downtown. The street lights cast a golden glow on the road, and the headlights from cars going the opposite direction make me squint. "Isn't it kind of late for a tattoo shop to be open?"

Lex flicks the blinker on and switches lanes to pass a car. "My artist, Scarlett, runs her own place and works by appointment only."

"And she has appointments after ten o'clock at night?" I peer out the window, watching the buildings and trees go by. "Wait." I turn my head in his direction. "Is she a vampire?"

Lex laughs. "Nah. She's just a kickass artist who makes her own schedule, which is lucky for me."

"Does she know about you?"

"What about me?" he asks in an amused tone. He knows exactly what I mean, so I shoot him a look, and he says, "Yes, she knows I'm a big, bad creature of the night." He laughs. "She's glamoured to keep my secret."

I nod. "Did she do the vines and roses on your arm?"

"Yep. She's done all of my ink in the last fifteen years or

so. Being immortal means having to find a new artist every handful of decades."

"Wouldn't it be easier just to turn one of them?" I ask without thinking. Of course that would mean taking their life away from them, but Lex and the others have already proven they're not above that. Case in point: me.

"Turning someone into a vampire isn't a small thing, Calla," Lex says, pulling off one of the downtown streets. We drive down a narrow alley between two buildings, barely big enough for his car. He slows to a stop where the alley opens up to a courtyard near the back of the buildings and kills the engine.

I catch my bottom lip between my teeth and pull at a loose thread on my shirt. "Will you tell me how it's done?"

"Why?" His voice has a lilt of amusement to it. "Are you thinking of joining the eternity club?"

My mouth goes dry, and I immediately shake my head. "I just... I was curious is all."

Lex drums his fingers against the steering wheel. "It's a process. There's a venom in our bite that needs to be coursing through your veins—along with our blood—when you die. You'd awaken weak and vulnerable, but once you drank human blood, you'd be stronger and faster than ever before. The first feed has to be directly from the vein, and a newbie vampire needs to drink so much blood to complete the transition that the human rarely survives."

My stomach clenches with unease. "That's intense," I say in a quiet voice, wiping my palms against my pants before glancing toward the brick building with a flickering neon red TATTOO sign in the window. "We should probably go in."

Lex watches me for a moment, his expression calculating, before he nods and gets out of the car. A second later, he opens my door and offers his hand. I take it and get out, and we walk across the dingy, dark courtyard to a large metal door. Lex bangs his fist against it a few times before opening it and ushering me inside.

My senses are overwhelmed by the sharp scent of antiseptic, which I guess is a good thing. The place is clean at least. I stay close to Lex but look around the small space. The walls are a deep red and mostly covered in tattoo sketches of all different sizes, some in color and others done in black ink. The floor is checkered tiles, and there's a brown couch directly to my right, under the window with the neon sign. Old rock music fills the room, and the fluorescent lighting along the exposed ceiling dims and brightens every few seconds.

A curvy woman with a blond pixie cut who looks to be in her late thirties based on the faint wrinkles around her eyes and mouth pushes aside a black curtain and steps into the room. She's wearing a black Rolling Stones T-shirt, ripped jeans, and white Doc Martens. "Lexington, you beautiful bastard, it's good to see you."

*Lexington?*

I arch a brow at him. "Is that your real name?"

He rolls his eyes, but his lips are curled into a grin. "Nope, but she's about to hold a needle against my skin, so she can call me whatever the hell she wants." Lex steps forward and pulls the woman into a hug. "What's new, Scar?" he asks, stepping back.

She shrugs, reaching behind an old wood counter, and the music quiets. "Not a damn thing." Her pale blue eyes slide to me, and I can't help but admire the dark purple makeup look she's rocking. "Who's this? You don't usually bring anyone when you come to visit me."

I force a smile, but something in my chest tightens at her words, and I'm not sure what to make of that. "I'm Calla. It's, um, nice to meet you."

She purses her bright red lips. "Hmm, okay, Calla." She looks me over. "You got any ink?"

"No," I tell her, "though I've always wanted to get something. I'm just not sure what."

She nods before turning her attention back to Lex. "Give me ten minutes. I'm almost set up."

"Thanks, Scar."

Scarlett disappears behind the curtain again, and I walk around the room, looking over the artwork on the walls. It's mostly skulls, flowers, and quotes, but mixed in are some more unique pieces with animals and languages I can't read. Scarlett is undeniably talented. No wonder Lex comes here.

Before long, she returns and leads us back to a small room with more art covering the walls and a black leather chair that reminds me of one you'd see in a dental office. There's a stool on wheels where Scarlet sits, pulling a tray over as Lex drops into the chair and swings his legs onto it.

I lean against the wall instead of taking the other rolling stool and watch the two of them chat softly as Scarlett pulls on black gloves. She preps the needle and picks up what I gather is a stencil, and Lex pulls his shirt off, flipping it over the back of the chair.

My eyes drop to his lean abs and end up stuck there. I swallow hard and press my lips together, forcing myself to tear my gaze away and instead focus on Scarlett as she presses the stencil to the left side of Lex's collarbone. She peels it away a moment later, leaving a black outline of vines that look as if they'll connect to the design that trails up his arm and over his shoulder. She hands him a mirror, and he nods at her before handing it back.

The buzz of the tattoo gun fills the room, and Lex grins at me.

"What?" I say.

"You don't need to stand all the way over there." He pats the stool next to him.

"I'm good." I'm curious about tattoos, sure, but I don't need to see the needle piercing his skin over and over at close range.

He pouts. "What if I want to hold your hand?"

Scarlett snorts.

"I think you'll live," I remark dryly.

Lex winks at me. "You think?"

I roll my eyes and push away from the wall, walking over and dropping onto the stool. "Baby," I mutter, slapping my hand onto the chair, palm up.

He slides his fingers through mine as Scarlett leans over and lowers the tattoo gun to his skin. The bastard doesn't even flinch. In fact, he inhales slowly and smiles as if he's at peace, and I faintly recall him saying that he enjoys pain. His thumb traces back and forth against my hand, and I watch that instead of the ink being permanently etched into his skin.

"So your thing is tattoos, Gabriel's is cooking, Kade's is… his hair, probably, and Atlas's is being the grumpiest person alive or undead or whatever." I panic and my gaze flies toward Scarlett before I remember what Lex said about glamouring her.

He chuckles. "You're mostly right."

I tilt my head. "What, Kade's thing isn't his hair?"

"No, you're definitely right about that. Atlas on the other hand…" Lex trails off, and I'm holding my breath waiting for him to give me some information that will help me make sense of the broody as hell vampire. "He was born to a very powerful vampire family a long, long time ago. There are certain expectations he's had to live with that would put a strain on anyone."

So Atlas wasn't turned, he was born a vampire. "Is that why the rest of you look up to him?"

"We respect him," Lex explains, holding my gaze as if Scarlett isn't in the room with us. "For many reasons. One of which being, for me at least, that he turned me. There's a special bond between a vampire and their sire. He doesn't control me, but he doesn't have to. I would do anything for him—we all would. And I see that look on your face, but before you say anything, you should know that he would do the same for us."

"Okay," I finally say. "But you're the only one he turned?"

Lex nods. "He saved my life. I was living in Brooklyn at the time, driving into the city for work. I left the office long after dark following a meeting that had run late one night and hit a whiteout storm. I was in a head-on collision and was minutes away from death when Atlas found me. He was driving in the opposite direction and saw the crash. I don't remember that night, just waking up several days later in Atlas's home on the Upper East Side with the most excruciating burning in my throat."

I swallow hard, my heart pounding in my chest. "I... I'm sorry that happened to you."

A flicker of surprise passes over his usually sharp features, softening the gray in his eyes. "Don't be," he says, squeezing my hand, "I'm not."

I wet my lips, nodding. "And what about the others? How did they become vampires?"

Lex glances over to Scarlett as she finishes tracing one of the thorns before turning his gaze back to me. "Kade was a vampire when Atlas and I met him shortly after I turned. He was going through some shit that he never really elaborated on, but he helped me get a handle on my bloodlust. I wasn't ready for the constant urge to rip into people's throats, so it was quite the adjustment."

"You still don't know how he became a vampire?"

He shakes his head. "And before you ask, I don't know about Gabriel either. It's not exactly something we talk about."

"Why not?" I ask, pulling my hand free from his and resting it in my lap.

He shrugs, and Scarlett snaps, "Don't move."

"Sorry, Scar." He clears his throat, then says to me, "Gabriel is a fairly private person, in case you hadn't noticed." The corner of his mouth kicks up. "I think it's just naturally ingrained in him for some reason."

I nod, feeling as if I've gotten to know my vampire housemates a little better—finally. I still have so many questions, most of which pertain to me and my future, but I suppose this is a start.

An hour later, Scarlett is bandaging Lex's new ink. She makes quick work of cleaning up her station and shrugs on a jacket. "I'm late for another appointment," she says, tossing a key at Lex, which he catches easily. "Lock up on your way out?"

"Sure thing."

She pushes through the curtain and disappears before I can say goodbye.

Lex makes no move to put his shirt back on and instead pokes at the bandage across his collarbone.

"Did it hurt?"

"I've felt worse," he answers. "It goes numb after a while."

"Oh."

He catches my chin and tilts my head up so we're at eye level. "I could give you one."

My pulse jackhammers. "What?" I squeak. "No way. Absolutely not."

Lex's deep laugher fills the small room, and he traces the

line of my jaw with his thumb. "I'm fully trained, Calla. I just don't ink myself."

I narrow my eyes and pull back instinctively, making his hand fall onto the armrest of the chair. "You're not getting anywhere near me with a tattoo gun, so don't even think about it."

"All right, all right," he concedes, grinning. "You know what I thought about while Scarlett was stabbing me a thousand times?"

"Oh, please do tell."

He lowers his voice and leans toward me, so close I can count the freckles across his cheeks and nose. "I thought about how badly I wanted to get you alone. How I would pin you to this chair and spread those gorgeous thighs of yours. How I would fuck you hard and fast, pounding your pussy until you screamed so loud anyone close enough to hear would think *you* were getting stabbed."

My voice is gone. I stare at him, at the glimmer of power in his wild eyes, and I can't bring myself to speak. Without thinking, I press my thighs together and lick the dryness from my lips. My breathing has gone shallow and my heart is beating in my throat.

"Come here," he says in a low voice.

I hesitate, but the look in his eyes paired with the insane fluttering in my stomach pushes me to move. I stand and swing my leg over the chair, straddling him as he grips my hips and settles me into his lap. I grab his shoulders to steady myself, and my breath catches when I feel him pressed against my core. I shift up slightly, and Lex groans in response, his fingers digging into my hips.

He trails his hands along my arms, then pushes my jacket off my shoulders. I lean back to pull it off the rest of the way and toss it behind me. Without warning, Lex tugs me forward, and I fall against his chest, pressing my hands into the chair on either side of him. His lips find mine in an instant, and he kisses me slowly, taking his time to explore the way my lips move with his as my eyes close of their own volition. His tongue darts out, and my lips part in a moan as he grips my hips again, grinding me against the hard thickness between his legs. His tongue sweeps into my mouth, dancing with mine as he tilts his head to deepen the kiss. I move my hips in slow circles, making my heart pound in my chest almost perfectly in time with the throbbing at the apex of my thighs.

Lex manages to move from underneath me and flip me onto my back, stealing the air from my lungs as I gasp in surprise. He traps me between his legs, his knees pressing into the chair on either side of me, and dives for my neck, kissing, licking, and sucking until my skin tingles. His fangs extend and scrape along my skin, gentle enough they don't slice into my throat but instead send a delicious shiver down my spine.

I reach between us and palm the front of his pants, desperate to feel him. When he groans, I pull his mouth back to mine and kiss him hard, telling him exactly what I want. I pop the button on his pants and tug the zipper down, pulling his cock out and running my hand down the shaft slowly.

"Calla," he growls against my lips.

I wrap my fingers around his velvet-soft length, moving my hand up and down at a lazy pace while our lips remain locked in a battle for control.

He pulls back, staring into my eyes as I continue to pump my hand on his cock. "You feel so good," he says in a husky tone, his gaze filled with liquid silver.

My cheeks feel hot and my pulse is pounding beneath my skin, but I don't stop. I pick up the pace, experimenting with my grip just a little, and Lex tips his head back, closing his eyes as his chest rises and falls faster.

"Don't you dare stop," he demands.

I grin, though he isn't looking at me. I move faster, then slow down, driving him crazy each time I switch paces.

"Christ," he grounds out, grabbing my hand and pulling it away from his cock. He traps both of my wrists above my head and presses his other hand against my stomach, sliding it past the waistband of my pants and finding the heat at my core. He pushes two fingers in easily, flicking my clit with his thumb. "You're a mess," he says in my ear, making me shiver. "I fucking love it." He nips my earlobe before pressing his lips to the pulse at my throat.

I suck in a breath and moan when he hits a particularly sensitive spot inside me. I tug on my wrists, wanting to touch him, but his grip is unforgiving. "Lex," I grumble, tugging again.

He kisses me chastely, pumping his fingers slowly and then picking up the pace as I did to him. "Yes, Calla?"

"How long are you going to keep—" My words break off as a wave of pleasure crashes over me, igniting an orgasm that vaults my hips off the chair as my pussy clenches around his fingers. *Holy shit.*

Lex smirks at me, fangs and all, and pulls his fingers out. He releases my wrists and curls his fingers around the waistband of my pants, tugging them along with my panties down to my knees.

Anticipation builds in my chest as I track his every move, and when he lines his cock up with my entrance, it takes everything in me not to thrust my hips and take him inside me.

He teases me, tracing my pussy lips with the blunt head of his cock, dipping inside a little more with each pass, until he seals his mouth over mine and thrusts all the way in.

I moan against his lips, squeezing my eyes shut as he pulls back and drives back into me. Once, twice, and then a third time. He slows his pace after that, letting me catch my breath as his lips move to my neck. I tense beneath him when his fangs sink into my skin, and I whimper as the sharp, split-second of pain morphs into warm, hazy pleasure. I melt, holding him against me and pushing my fingers through his hair as he drinks deeply and rolls his hips, hitting a spot so deep, I see stars behind my eyelids.

His pace quickens as he pulls away from my neck, licking the puncture marks until they stop bleeding. "You are my new favorite taste." He brushes his lips against mine in a whisper of a kiss, and his words make my chest tighten with a foreign sensation that I have no time to decipher.

I open my eyes to meet his gaze, and the second I do, another orgasm rips through me, stealing my breath as I grind my hips against him, reveling in the friction between us.

"That a girl," Lex murmurs, slowing his thrusts, but continues moving inside me as I come down from my euphoric high. "Catch your breath, because I'm not done with you yet."

That sparks something in me, and I lift my hips to urge him on. Evidently, I'm not done with him either.

His thrusts become fast and hard, until he pulls out completely and flips me over. "Wrap your arms around the chair," he orders, spreading my legs as I move to obey him. He takes me from behind, making my pussy clench around him, and I gasp when hits even deeper inside me at this angle.

"Lex," I breathe, and I'm not sure if it's a prayer or a curse at this point.

He pounds into me, breathing harder. "Hold on."

My entire world narrows on the sensations flooding through me, and everything comes crashing down at once. I cry out with my third release, and Lex grunts, stiffening inside me as his own climax reaches a crescendo. He pulls out and we end up curled against one another, our labored breathing filling the small room with heat and the smell of sex.

Lex rests his forehead against mine, brushing his fingers along my cheek. "You good?" he checks.

I only nod, because I'm not sure my voice will work at this point. I softly trace the outline of his new bandage with my finger before meeting his gaze.

He licks his lips, then grins at me. "That is officially my favorite tattoo."

## 11

When we return to the house, I slip away to my bathroom and start filling the soaker tub with water. I need something to clear my head, and a hot bath filled with oils and bubbles seems like the perfect fix. I'm still going to talk to Gabriel, but I need some time to myself first.

I get undressed, dropping my clothes on the marble floor, then step into the tub and ease myself into the soapy, spearmint and eucalyptus scented water.

The room is hazy with steam, and I sigh, closing my eyes and leaning my head back against the plush cushion. My core aches from the extra time Lex and I spent at the tattoo shop, but it's a pleasant ache. One of satisfaction and one I very much want to experience again.

It's only once I've completely relaxed, the tension literally melting out of my body, that the thought smacks me in the face.

I don't really hate it here.

As much as I should—as much as I *want* to, I don't. I can't pinpoint when it happened, but I don't have the immediate urge to attempt an escape the moment I'm alone. I've only been here four days, so that's a little—or a lot—embarrassing, but maybe it's the part of me that knows it's useless to run. They'll find me and drag me back here and it will all be for nothing.

I guess I should be grateful they're allowing me some semblance of normal in letting me continue to go to class, even after what happened with Brighton this morning.

Now, I just need to find out *why*. There are so many whys, and the more I think about it and try to figure them out, the more my head spins and pounds with tension.

"Calla?" Gabriel's voice floats in from the bedroom, and my body flushes with heat. It could be from the temperature of the water, but the safer bet would be that it's what Gabriel's voice does to me.

"In here," I call without thinking, pressing my lips together. Oddly enough, I'm not nervous about him seeing me naked.

He steps into the room and his eyes immediately find me. "That looks relaxing." His gaze trails along the length of my soapy body as he wets his lips. Evidently, he's not concerned about subtlety.

I close my eyes, feeling warmer under his gaze. "Hmm, it is really nice."

His shoes make little sound as he walks closer, and I open my eyes, turning my head just as he kneels at the side of the tub. The sight has me biting my lip as his eyes flick between mine.

"Did—" I clear my throat. "Did you need something?"

The corner of his mouth lifts and he hooks his finger under my chin, tilting my head up a little. "Seeing you like this is exactly what I need."

I lift my hand out of the water and run it up his chest

until I reach his neck, where I curl my fingers and pull him closer. "Kiss me?" I whisper.

His mouth covers mine in an instant, soft but hungry. Our lips battle for control, and I tug at the hair at the back of his neck as one of his hands grips the side of the tub and the other slips under the water. I gasp into his mouth when he pinches my nipple, and he chuckles softly.

I pull back a little, trailing my lips along his jaw. "I'm sorry you were upset before dinner," I murmur, kissing the corner of his mouth. "You can talk to me, you know."

His fingers slide down my chest, and my breath hitches when he reaches my navel. "You're sweet," he says in a soft voice. "I don't need to burden you with these things."

"I know that," I assure him, "but you can, is what I'm saying."

He kisses the tip of my nose and smiles at me. "Thank you."

I mirror his smile, blushing hotly when his fingers delve lower until they brush my mound. "Gabriel…"

His gaze is locked on mine. "Tell me what you need, angel."

"You," I breathe, my chest rising and falling a little quicker now. "Just… you."

He holds my gaze as he pushes two fingers inside me, stealing the breath from my lungs when he curls them and rubs my clit with his thumb. "Relax," he murmurs, and I breathe out slowly, forcing my muscles to unclench. "That's it."

I open my legs as wide as I can in the tub and moan. "Why do I get the feeling this is a distraction for you as much as it is for me?"

"Don't worry about me," he says, picking up the pace as he leans in and presses his lips to the side of my neck.

I tilt my head slightly, an invitation, but he just keeps

kissing and sucking playfully. "I do, though," I murmur, and while my motive for the conversation isn't that, I do still care about him. I open my mouth to speak, but all that comes out is another moan when he hits a sensitive spot. He grins against my skin, his tongue darting out to flick along my neck as he rubs that same spot over and over, driving me to new heights of pleasure, to the point I almost forget what I'm trying to do.

"I just don't like seeing you upset," I say in a quiet voice, arching my hips to push his fingers deeper.

He circles my clit with his thumb, again increasing the speed of his fingers. "Calla—"

I'm close. My nerves are vibrating with energy, and the pressure building between my legs is going to explode any second.

"Does it have to do with me being here? With all the secrets?"

Gabriel pulls away from my neck, and his fingers still inside of me. "What?" His eyes search my face, and I fight the urge to look away, as if I've been caught doing something wrong.

"I..."

He pulls his fingers out and shifts back. "What are you asking me? Truly?" His forehead is creased and his jaw is set tight. I don't like this look on him. Even more, I don't like that I'm the reason he's looking at me like that.

"N-nothing. I want to make sure you're okay. You've been looking out for me, and—"

"And you thought I would share the information you haven't been able to gather on your own."

"No," I lie, "I... Never mind."

Silence stretches between us, and I no longer feel all warm and fuzzy. I cross my arms to cover my breasts, wanting to get out of the water.

"What do you want to know?" His voice is low, flat. It's not unkind, but it also doesn't hold its usual warmth that I've grown accustomed to and that has been known to bring me comfort.

I glance around the luxurious space, biting the inside of my cheek. This could be my only opportunity to get some information, but the way he's looking at me has made me unable to grasp the questions I want to ask.

Gabriel exhales heavily and stands. "Next time you want to use me, I'd prefer you be upfront about it." He walks out of the bathroom without another word, and I'm equal parts shocked and embarrassed at the sting of tears in my eyes.

---

After the epic failure that left me without answers, I'm glad to be on campus all day. Between back-to-back classes and a study session after lunch, my day is full of normal, human things. Time away from the house—and the guys—will do me good. I need to clear my head and refocus so I can make a plan—a *better* plan than last night—to figure this shit out.

Brighton meets me at the coffee cart we frequent on campus in between my second lecture and our study session. We're in different programs but find that studying together keeps us both focused better. We deemed this particular coffee cart as our favorite last year. It's cheaper than Starbucks and pretty much tastes the same. Plus, it's right on campus, so it gets extra points for easy access.

"I got your favorite," she says cheerily, holding up a black paper cup.

I shoot her a grin as I reach for the peppermint mocha and take a sip, sighing in content as warmth floods through me. "This is why I love you."

She snorts, tossing her strawberry blond waves over her

shoulder, and takes a drink from her iced latte. Brighton is of the opinion that iced coffee is for all year round, even if there's snow on the ground, which we're not far past. She's bundled up in an emerald peacoat with rosy cheeks from the cold wind, but even still, you won't see her ordering a hot latte. "How was class?" she asks.

I shrug as we start walking along the cobblestone path toward the campus library. "Same old," I tell her, feeling a little uncomfortable chatting normally after what happened yesterday. She doesn't remember, of course, but I do.

Brighton nods. "Oh hey, sorry I had to miss brunch yesterday. I had the worst headache when I got up."

I wave her off, ignoring the pit of guilt in my stomach. "No need to apologize."

"I guess I can't party as hard as we did in first year," she says, winking at me.

I laugh, taking another sip of my drink. "Guess not."

We meet up with a few other friends and get to studying. I'm bouncing between my Sociological Theory textbook, reading and making notes on the legal pad next to me, and the assigned articles for my Law and Society class. It doesn't take long for me to get immersed in my studies, and even the sound of conversation around me becomes white noise.

When I reach the end of my last article, I close my book and cap my pen, sighing. I rub my eyes and glance around the library. Most of the students have packed up and left, including everyone at our table besides Brighton and me. I hadn't even noticed when the others left us.

"Damn," I mumble, checking my phone for the time. We've been working for almost four hours. The sky is getting dark outside, making the space feel cozy compared to the wind blowing the trees across campus.

"You went to this whole other place," Brighton teases without glancing up from her phone. She's scrolling on

Instagram with her textbook open in front of her. "Anyway," she says, slipping her phone into her bag before flipping her book closed, "we should get going."

I nod and pack up my things before we head out of the library.

"I'm parked across campus," she says as we push through the double doors outside. "You want a ride?"

The wind knocks the air out of me, and I hug my jacket closer. "Oh, that's okay, I—"

"Calla."

I freeze at the sound of Atlas's voice and turn around to find him leaning against the building. He's wearing a black coat with a high collar, and that paired with the rest of his outfit and the annoyingly handsome way his hair is styled makes him look like he just walked off the set of a GQ magazine shoot.

My jaw clenches tight as he pushes off the building and walks toward us.

"Who is that?" Brighton asks in a whisper, her eyes wide and filled with curiosity.

"Nobody," I say quickly, turning to stand in front of her and put my back to him. "Listen, I—"

Brighton sidesteps me and closes the rest of the distance between us and Atlas. I whip around as she puts on that charming smile of hers and sticks her hand out. "Hi," she says cheerily, "I'm Brighton, Calla's B-F-F."

Just when I think I might see Atlas smile for the first time, he only nods, reaching out to shake Brighton's hand.

"Erm, okay," she says, pulling her hand back and flicking an awkward glance at me before saying, "Calla's never mentioned you before."

I step in quickly. "Uh, yeah. Atlas is a… family friend." The words taste bitter on my tongue. "He just recently moved here, and I've been showing him around a bit."

Lying to my best friend is just the cherry on this giant crap cake.

The curiosity in her gaze quickly turns to interest as she looks between us. "That's cool," she says, shooting me a wink that I think is supposed to be sneaky but is definitely not missed by the vampire standing in front of us. Brighton turns her attention to Atlas. "So if you're new here, that means you probably don't know about the St. Patrick's Day party this weekend."

He arches a brow, pursing his lips. "No, I don't."

She perks up even more at that, practically batting her lashes at him. If I wasn't so annoyed at Atlas showing up here and ambushing me with Brighton, I would almost think it was funny. "You definitely need to come. Calla and I go every year. It's a fucking blast."

I open my mouth to tell her that I don't really feel like going this year, but before I can get the words out, Atlas speaks up.

"Sounds fun. I'll be there."

I blink at him in surprise. Since I met Atlas last week, he hasn't seemed like the social type, even among the guys. He'll contribute to some conversations, sure, but he doesn't go out of his way to initiate them. Most of the time, he fits the broody and quiet persona to a T. My eyes narrow; he has to be up to something, or this is just another way to show his control over me.

Atlas shifts his attention to me. "Are you ready to go?"

"Sure," I answer, glancing at Brighton. "I'll talk to you tomorrow?"

"Uh-huh," she says, her tone suggestive as she looks back and forth between Atlas and me.

I shake my head at her before she starts walking across the lawn toward the other side of campus, leaving me to turn and face Atlas.

"Your friend is very... enthusiastic."

I cross my arms, glaring at him. "What the hell was that?"

He cocks his head to the side, watching me. "What was what, Calla?" He sounds irritated by my question, but I'm the one with a reason to be pissed off.

"You showing up here," I say, shaking my head. "Kade messed with her head to make her forget me telling her about you, then you—"

"Her knowing I exist is far off from her knowing you are living with a house full of vampires." His condescending tone makes me scowl.

"Whatever. Let's just go."

I half-expect him to say something more that will only add fuel to the fire in my chest, but he just nods and starts walking. I follow him to the parking lot without a word and get into his Escalade, which looks wildly out of place in the student parking lot. I get in the passenger seat and tuck my bag between my legs, staring out the windshield as Atlas starts the car and drives out of the lot.

"Am I to expect a vampire chauffeur every day, or...?"

"It's dark, and I didn't want you taking a cab," is all he says.

My brows knit, because his words almost make it sound as if he cares about my safety. "Okay," I finally say. "Well, I don't have class tomorrow, so you don't have to worry about picking me up."

"I know."

I press my lips together, frowning at his detached tone. "Right."

Atlas turns onto one of the main roads, tapping his fingers against the steering wheel. "Are you hungry? Gabriel and Kade are out for the night, and Lex already ate, so we can stop somewhere."

"Oh, um, I'm okay." The ball of nerves in my stomach

from Atlas and Brighton meeting effectively ruined my appetite. "I mean, unless you're hungry?"

He casts me a sideways glance. "I'm always hungry, but I'm afraid a Chick-fil-A drive-thru won't satisfy my cravings."

Heat floods my cheeks, and I try to ignore the meaning behind his words, but I can't deny the way my pulse races at the thought of him... *Nope. Don't go there.* "I don't know, their waffle fries are pretty good." Despite the upset from earlier, my stomach grumbles.

He exhales on a laugh. "I thought you weren't hungry."

I shrug, though he's focusing on the road now. "I'll eat when we get back to the house. I'm sure there's some leftover lasagna. Gabriel made enough to feed an army."

Atlas nods. "He does that. It makes him feel like he's taking care of his family."

"He's a good guy," I say without hesitation. It's a truth I believe wholeheartedly, which makes me feel a tinge of guilt over what I tried to do last night.

It's as if Atlas is able to read my mind, because he says, "You should try apologizing to him. He cares about you, so I'm sure he'll be forgiving."

My stomach drops. "You know?"

"I'm surprised you resorted to seduction for information so quickly," he says, answering my question with a jab that makes me not want to look at him. *Asshole.*

I inhale slowly before replying, "Well, the four of you don't exactly make it easy to get information otherwise."

"Hmm, and how did your tactic work out?" he asks, turning off the main road onto our street.

"Go to hell," I shoot back, unbuckling my belt the second we pull into the driveway.

Atlas pulls into a spot in the garage, shifting the car into park, and when I open the door, he moves faster than my eyes can follow and pulls it shut.

"Wha—"

"You will know what we want you to know, when we want you to know it." His voice is low, threatening, and his face is so close I feel the warmth of his breath on my cheek.

Instead of backing down, I blurt, "What if I can help?" When he arches a brow, I add, "I mean, if I can—if I help you with whatever 'business acquisitions' you're talking about, will you let me out of this damn contract?"

He leans back a little, his arm still braced on the console between us, and glances out the windshield. I wait, but he doesn't say anything.

"I'm not going to be a slave my entire life," I snap, breaking the silence, and Atlas looks my way again. "If that's all you want me for, you may as well kill me now because I'm not going to be complacent." My heart pounds against my chest almost painfully as I wait for him to respond. I'm fully expecting him to threaten to *make* me complacent, which is a very real possibility, but again, he says nothing. *Fuck this*.

I push the door open and climb out of the Escalade before storming into the house, and I don't stop moving until I'm on the other side of my bedroom door. I collapse against it, my breathing shallow.

At this point, I've played all my cards. Whatever game this is, I have most definitely lost.

## 12

The following morning, I wake with a weight on my chest that has me feeling anxious and cagey. Going from working out daily to not working out in almost a week has taken a toll on me physically and mentally. I need to move, to exert some energy.

I tie my hair up and change into a matching black sports bra and high-waisted legging set before shoving my feet into my running shoes and grabbing my phone off the charger on the table beside the bed.

It's barely after seven, so I grab a heavy gray sweater from the closet, tugging it on over my head, then search my book bag until I find my wireless headphones.

After sticking them in my ears, I pocket my phone and jog downstairs to leave for a run around the neighborhood. If I'm lucky, none of the guys will be awake yet, or will have already left for work.

No such luck.

Gabriel is sitting at the kitchen counter, sipping an espresso while reading from his tablet.

My eyes quickly shift to the window… where it's pouring

rain outside. When the hell did that start? The forecast didn't call for rain.

"Morning," I say in a small voice as I open the fridge and grab a bottle of water.

"Morning," he echoes softly. "Were you planning to go for a run?"

I close the fridge and nod, uncapping the bottle. "It's just rain."

"It's also freezing out." He sets his tablet on the counter. "Why don't you check out the gym here instead?"

I freeze with the water bottle halfway to my lips. "You guys have a gym? Why is this the first I'm hearing of it?"

"You didn't ask," he offers.

I frown at that. "Okay. Where is it?"

"It's above the garage." He nods toward the door we came in when I first arrived last week. "There's a door to the stairwell that leads up to it."

My heart races with excitement. If I'd known they had workout equipment, I would've been using it every day since I got here. I screw the lid back on my water bottle and make my way toward the garage. Pausing, I turn back toward the kitchen. "Thanks, Gabriel. And, um, about last night... I-I'm sorry." The words are out of my mouth before I can stop them. The apology is genuine, but it tastes sour on my tongue and I'm not sure why.

He nods, smiling a little before picking his tablet back up.

A bit of the weight on my chest over last night eases as I make my way toward the garage. I jog up the stairs after finding the door easily enough and stop dead at the top of the landing when my eyes land on a bare-chested Atlas. My mouth goes dry, and the water bottle almost slips out of my hand as I openly gawk at him.

He either hasn't noticed me yet—doubtful—or he's ignoring me and choosing to focus on the massive amount of weight he's benching. It has to be at least two hundred pounds, which leads my mind to wander... He could lift *me*. Parts of me like the thought of that way too much.

Atlas returns the barbell to the rack and sits up. "Are you planning to stand there and watch me the entire time?" He swings his leg over the bench and looks at me. His hair is falling into his face, the ends damp with sweat. He pushes it back and stands, arching a brow at me as he closes the distance between us.

It takes far more effort than I care to admit to pull my gaze from his chiseled stomach and meet his silver gaze. "I..." I clear my throat and try again. "I was going to go for a run, but it's raining and cold."

He nods. "Cardio machines are back there." He jerks his thumb behind him, and for the first time since I stepped into the room, I take a look around.

For a home gym, the space is impressive. It doesn't surprise me at this point, and in this case, I'm practically giddy over how fancy it is. The wall across the room is made of windows where the different cardio machines are lined up, looking out to the side of the property that's filled with trees. There's a treadmill, an elliptical, and one of those ridiculously expensive spin bikes with the giant screen attached.

I walk around a bit, the padded floor soft under my running shoes. The other walls are a muted gray, and track lighting runs along the ceiling. The room is cold, which is preferable when working up a sweat. I pass by a mini-fridge against the wall next to the bench press Atlas was using and set my water bottle on it as I continue around the room. It's a simple layout: cardio machines and stretching mats at one end and weight racks and benches at the other. There's plenty of open space in the center of the room and mirrors on the wall adjacent to the door I came in through.

"What do you usually do?"

I jump at the sound of Atlas's voice so close to my ear and whip around to face him, taking a healthy step back before looking up at him. "Cardio to warm up," I tell him, "and then weight lifting until I can barely walk or lift my arms."

He purses his lips. "And you did this—"

"Every day," I answer.

I'm not sure why I'm surprised at how impressed he looks, but it makes me press my lips together against a smile.

"I, uh… I've been training vigorously since the day my parents told me about the agreement." I laugh humorlessly. "As if I could somehow fight my way out of it." Shaking my head as heat floods my cheeks, I add, "I don't know why I'm telling you this."

Atlas steps closer, and I can feel the heat radiating from him. Before he can say anything, though, I speak again.

"I was willing to fight for my freedom. To train and work hard every single day so that…" I shake my head again, mostly at myself. "Forget it."

"Calla—"

"The moment I stepped into my apartment the night you came for me, I knew. No amount of training would have been enough."

"Your dedication to protecting yourself is admirable."

I shrug. "My family certainly wasn't going to." They *couldn't*. Because how exactly do you prevent four vampires from taking what they believe to be entitled to?

His gaze holds. "What's your reason for training now?"

Another shrug. "Maybe I'm going to stab you again," I offer, "gotta keep my strength up."

I'm kidding—mostly—but when he doesn't so much as crack a smile, I cringe inwardly.

"Fine. It's a… release. It feels good to push my body, to test the limits of my endurance." It can also be a really good distraction, which, these days, could most definitely come in handy.

Atlas nods as if he understands what I'm feeling, as if he's felt it too. "Fight me."

I scratch the back of my neck, suddenly feeling a hell of a lot more self-conscious having my hair pulled up off my neck with his silver eyes trained on my every movement. "Huh?" I must've heard him wrong. Surely, he isn't saying—

"Fight. Me." He repeats the words slowly. Pointedly. Then adds, "No weapons."

That stirs something in me, and I cross my arms over my chest. "Fine." There aren't any weapons in my sightline anyway. I meet his gaze and say, "No vampire mojo."

He presses his lips into a thin line. Ha. He's trying not to smile. "You think I need that?"

I tilt my head back and forth. "I don't know. Seems pretty convenient that you can touch or look at your opponent and make them do whatever you say. It's kind of cheating if you think about it." My tone is slightly mocking; I'm baiting him. A dangerous game, but it makes my stomach swirl with excitement.

One second I'm staring into his eyes, and the next I'm looking at the ceiling, my back pressed against the mat with the air knocked out of me.

I suck in a breath and grumble, "Cheater."

Atlas hovers over me, holding himself up with one hand, while the other has both of my wrists trapped above my head. My heart is pounding in my chest, and the heat pooling much lower gives away that I don't particularly dislike the position I'm in. Damn him.

He stands, pulling me up with him in a blur of motion. The room spins for a second before my vision rights itself, and I launch myself at him without hesitation. My fist connects with his jaw, and I just barely manage to duck under his arm when he grabs for me again. I spin around and kick hard, catching him in the back. He stumbles forward a couple of steps before rolling his shoulders back and turning to face me.

"You've got strength behind you. That's good."

I exhale a breathy laugh. "For what exactly?"

He advances again, this time without using his preternatural speed. Even still, he catches me off guard and pushes me back until I collide with the wall next to the bench press. Atlas traps my wrists against the wall above my head and slowly leans in until the tip of his nose grazes mine.

"Being a human in our world is very dangerous," he says in a low voice, though I don't think he's threatening me.

I lift my knee, trying to catch him between the legs, but he manages to turn fast enough that I hit his thigh instead. I attempt to pull my wrists free, but it's useless. I can train all I want, I'll never have the strength to overpower a vampire. "What's your point, Atlas?"

His eyes flare with something I haven't seen from him before—lust. The fire there makes my breath catch, and when he leans back enough for me to see his face and drags his tongue along his bottom lip, I can't keep my eyes from going there. "You're safe here," he says, his voice barely above a whisper. "From outside dangers, at least."

I swallow hard. "Not from you?"

His eyes darken, and when he opens his mouth to respond, his fangs flash. Warmth pools in my belly at the thought of him pressing into me and sinking his teeth into my neck.

His jaw snaps shut, clenching sharply before he says, "Don't look at me like that." There's a warning in his voice that I choose to ignore.

"Like what?" I push.

His upper lip curls, and he leans in once more, his chest

brushing mine as he speaks low into my ear. "Like you want me to take you right here against this wall. With my fangs and my cock."

Heat flares in my cheeks, and I close my eyes, my pulse ticking faster, like a bomb about to detonate. "What do *you* want?" I ask in a soft voice, pressing my thighs together, trying to ease the ache throbbing between them.

He laughs darkly. "What I want, Calla..." His lips graze my jaw and his grip on my wrists tightens. "You wouldn't survive it."

His words should terrify me. I should be using every bit of strength I have to fight him off and run away.

Instead, I turn my head and press my lips against his cheek.

He blinks at me in surprise.

"I'm not as breakable as you think," I tell him, "and I don't think you're as vicious as you'd like me to believe."

Those silver eyes narrow ever so slightly. "Are you sure you'd like to take a gamble on that?"

I shrug. "What do I have to lose? Truly?"

His expression softens, and he frees my wrists, though he doesn't move away. He snags my chin, tilting my head back to meet his gaze. "You are not at all what I was expecting," he admits.

Arching a brow, I ask, "What *were* you expecting?"

He purses his lips. "Fear."

Huh. I guess my bravado is better than I thought.

"Do... do you want me to fear you?"

"Yes." There is no hesitation in his response.

A shiver runs through me, and I lick the dryness from my lips seconds before his fingers side from my chin to wrap around my throat. He isn't squeezing, but he's using enough pressure to keep me against the wall.

"I want to tear into your throat and devour your blood. I

want to see the moment you realize you are completely powerless against me. And more than anything, I want to feel that delicious moment of surrender when the last ounce of fight leaves your body and you give yourself to me."

*Holy fucking shit.*

I am completely frozen. I couldn't move even if he didn't have his fingers wrapped around my throat. My heart is pounding against my ribcage, desperate to escape. I've never been so scared and excited in my life, and if I had to bet, that's written all over my face.

Atlas's thumb brushes along my jaw, slow and gentle. "You should go." His voice is hard, reserved.

I blink at him, unable to form words. Part of me is tempted to push him further, to test his resolve and challenge his words, but apparently there's a thread of self-preservation left in me, because when he lets me go and steps away, I hurry for the door and don't stop moving until I'm locked in the bathroom connected to my room.

I stare at my reflection. My cheeks and chest are flushed, and I'm breathing hard, as if I've just finished the run I wanted to go on this morning.

I press my hand over my heart and count the rapid beats until they slow to a normal pace, then I shake my head at my reflection.

"I am so screwed."

## 13

Two days later, my mind is still reeling from my encounter with Atlas. I've steered clear of him around the house, using the gym above the garage late at night or when I know he's gone for a while.

I'd like to think it's because I'm scared of the vampire, but really, I'm scared of what I want him to do to me. Everything he said the other day has me all twisted up inside.

I increase the speed of the treadmill and turn up my music, running in time with the beat.

My phone buzzes with messages—Brighton's been texting me since I got out of class a few hours ago—but I ignore them, focusing on the rhythm of my shoes hitting the treadmill.

I groan and stop the machine when my music cuts off from an incoming call. I answer it on speakerphone. "Brighton you have got to chill," I say in between breaths.

"Jesus, Cal. What are you doing?" Her voice teases at innuendo, and I roll my eyes, reaching for my water.

"I was *trying* to work out," I say, downing half the bottle.

"What are you wearing tonight?"

"Huh?" I ask, wiping the sweat from my forehead with the back of my hand.

"The St. Patrick's Day party?" She sighs. "I've been texting you about it all afternoon."

"I know," I grumble.

"It's tonight."

"So?"

"What do you mean *so*?" she whines. "Aren't you going to bring that hottie friend of yours? Because if you're not interested, I sure as hell am."

I cringe. When it comes to Atlas, I have no idea what I am. Dangerously attracted to him? Definitely. Scared of what that means? Hell to the yes. I shake my head, though Brighton can't see me. "Yeah, I don't think I'm going to go."

She laughs. "You're cute. I'm ordering an Uber and picking you up at nine."

My stomach drops. Kade said he'd told her that I moved, but I really don't want to be put in a position where she starts asking questions about it that I can't answer. "No," I say quickly. "I mean, I'll just meet you there. Can you text me the address?"

"Ugh, you're going to show up with a hot piece of ass, and I'll be arriving solo."

"And ready to prowl," I tease, getting off the treadmill. I didn't finish my workout, but I'm quickly losing the motivation to exert myself right now.

"You know it." There's yelling in the background, but I can't make out the words. "Shit," she grumbles, "I gotta go, babe. I'll see you later."

I frown, grabbing my water bottle to take back in the house. "Hang on. Is everything okay?"

"Oh yeah, just the usual super-fun family drama. Nothing I can't handle. And by handle, I mean ignore."

"I'm sorry, Bri," I say softly.

"This shit makes me understand your decision to leave New York on a whole other level."

Of course she doesn't know the whole truth, just that I left after irreconcilable differences with my family. That was putting it lightly, but without getting into the gritty details, which included the four vampires I'm now stuck living with, it was really the best I could do.

"Can I do anything?"

"You already are. I'll see you tonight!" With that, she disconnects the call, and I jump when my music starts blaring again. I turn it down and head down the stairs, through the garage—Atlas's black Escalade is in its spot—and back into the house.

I stop in the kitchen to find something to eat. It's not quite late enough for dinner, but I need something to hold me over until then, because my stomach won't stop grumbling.

I search through the fridge and pantry and settle on a bright green apple with crunchy peanut butter and some tortilla chips. Sitting at the kitchen counter munching on my snacks, I scroll through this week's discussion thread for my Urban Studies class on my phone, adding a few comments under my classmates' posts.

I'm washing my dishes when Lex walks in from the garage, whistling what I think is an Eminem song. He shoots me a wink as he approaches, then leans against the counter. "Atlas tells me we're going to a party tonight."

I close the dishwasher and spin around to look at him. "What?" Shaking my head, I say, "No way. I'm not going to show up to a college party with an entourage of vampires. It's not happening."

He grins. "You going to tell that to Atlas?"

My jaw clenches, and I roll my eyes. "I'll—"

"Tell me what?"

I clamp my mouth shut when his voice reaches me, and turn to look at him. He's arching a brow, waiting for me to answer.

"Calla doesn't want us crashing her party," Lex says, and I don't have to look at him to know he's grinning.

"It's bad enough *you're* coming," I tell Atlas. "How do you think it's going to look if I show up with all of you?"

"Uh, it's going to look like you're the luckiest woman in this fucking city," Kade chimes in as he struts into the room.

*Where did he come from?*

"This is ridiculous," I grumble.

Lex slides his arm around my waist and pulls me against his side, pressing his lips to my ear. "Come on," he murmurs, "it'll be fun."

I'm leaning into him before I can stop myself. "I don't believe that for a second," I say in a low voice.

"I'll make you a deal." He rests his chin on the top of my head. "You don't make a fuss about tonight, and Atlas will do whatever your heart desires."

My stomach clenches at the thought of having the typically stoic vampire at *my* mercy. I can't bring myself to look at him, though he must hear the sound of my pulse racing beneath my flushed skin.

Kade chuckles. "Can I get in on that?"

Atlas rolls his eyes. "Not in your lifetime."

"You little liar," Kade shoots back, eyes glimmering with amusement.

My interest is officially piqued. I shiver at the thought of Kade having his way with Atlas as he did me. Or would Atlas overpower him and take control?

"Fine," I say, refocusing and shifting away from Lex. He lets me, of course, otherwise I wouldn't be able to move. "But you guys better act fucking normal."

Lex grins when he realizes I directed that last bit at him.

"I'm going to shower," I say with a sigh and walk toward the hallway to my bedroom.

"Want some company?" Kade calls after me.

"Not even a little bit," I say automatically without turning back.

"I'm surrounded by liars." His voice carries to me as I close the bedroom door.

---

Arriving at the address Brighton texted me a few hours ago, my Docs crunch against the gravel driveway when I slide out of the backseat of the Escalade. I adjust the knee-length, silk emerald dress that rode up my thighs during the drive across the city. I shiver at the chill in the air and wrap my arms around myself as the guys get out of the car. I'm vibrating with nervous energy and can barely wait to get inside and get a drink in my hand.

Kade, Lex, Gabriel, and Atlas don't exactly exude subtlety. They're wildly attractive and intimidating, and showing up with the four of them flanking me has my heart pounding like a jackhammer. People are going to stare and whisper and make assumptions. Brighton will have a million questions that I won't be able to answer.

"Relax, angel," Gabriel says in my ear.

I force a smile. "I'm fine. Let's just get this over with."

Kade rolls his eyes from my other side. "So dramatic. It's a party, not an execution."

Music booms from the farmhouse at the end of the driveway, the heavy bass making the ground vibrate. Twinkle lights are strung across the front porch, and the air is filled with a heady combination of pot smoke and booze.

I shoot Brighton a quick text to let her know I'm here as the five of us approach the house. I'm not even sure who lives here; the St. Patrick's Day party changes location every year. Not that it matters. There are so many people here, most of which are complete strangers to me and to each other.

The second we step inside, I'm sucked into the chaotic atmosphere. Students are dancing and singing at the top of their lungs to pop music that blares from a couple of massive speakers in what I would assume is normally a living room off to the right of the entryway. There are green balloons and streamers hung everywhere, and most of the partygoers are either dressed in green like me, or have on hats or different bright green headpieces.

I turn to tell the guys that I'm going to find Brighton—and a drink—only to find that Lex and Kade have already disappeared into the crowd. Part of me is relieved I won't have to explain them to my best friend, but another part of me is nervous they're loose in a house full of people.

Atlas lingers slightly behind me to the left, glancing around the crowd of people and looking wholly disinterested by the entire event.

I bite my tongue to keep from telling him that he should have stayed home. My head turns toward Gabriel when he places his hand against my lower back.

He leans in, grazing the shell of my ear with his lips and sending a shiver down my spine. "Drink?"

I fight the urge to lean into him and close my eyes. Everything about Gabriel makes me want to wrap myself in him, and I'm still trying to figure that out. "Sure," I say, "anything is fine."

"I don't think there will be much of a variety at a frat party," Atlas chimes in, glancing at me from where he's leaning against the wall.

I prop my hands on my hips. "You look like someone's

dad who's about to bust in and break up the party," I tell him, "just so you know."

His eyes narrow, and my stomach dips in response. "And shall I tell you what you look like in that dress?" There's a thinly veiled challenge in his tone, one I can't help but take the bait for.

"Please do."

Atlas pushes away from the wall and closes the short distance between us. I stand my ground, but my pulse races when I realize that Gabriel slipped away to get our drinks.

*He couldn't save you from me, anyway*, the dark expression on Atlas's face says.

Before I have a chance to react, Atlas manages to back me up against the wall next to the living room. We're tucked into an alcove between the other room and a staircase. To any onlooker, it would likely appear as if we're a couple trying to find a more private spot, but the race in my pulse tells a different story.

"You're nervous," he says in a low voice, dipping his face so his lips are close to my ear. "Do I make you nervous, Calla?"

I close my eyes as my name rolls off his tongue, and my head tips back against the wall. I want to open my mouth and tell him no, but he'll know I'm lying the second the word leaves my lips. Instead, I turn my face away, exposing my neck. I wore my hair in dark brown curls, pulled away from my face in a high pony. Was it to taunt the guys while we're here tonight? There's a pretty good chance.

I swallow hard, wishing Gabriel would hurry back with that drink. "You make me a lot of things."

Atlas presses closer, and heat floods through me at the hard contact of his body against mine. His hands are flat against the wall on either side of me; I'm caged in with nowhere to go. "What about right now?"

I turn my head to meet his gaze and lose myself in the inhuman color of his irises. I guess they could be mistaken for a really light shade of blue, but not up this close. "Right now..." I echo, feeling bold even as the alarm bells blare in my head. "Right now, you make me want to find the first empty room in this house and let you make me forget why I should hate you."

He tilts his head to the side, staring into my eyes, and I have the fleeting thought that he's about to kiss me. My stomach swirls with nerves and excitement, and the heat between my legs is a pulsing reminder of what my body desperately desires.

I catch a glimpse of Gabriel over Atlas's shoulder and my stomach clenches at the thought of the three of us.

"Not here," Atlas finally says.

When he moves back, my stomach drops, and I try to hide the disappointment weighing heavy in my chest by smiling at Gabriel and taking the red Solo cup he hands me.

"It's some sort of hard lemonade," he tells me, handing a cup to Atlas before taking a drink from the remaining one in his hand.

"Have you seen the others?" I ask, sipping the drink. I grimace at the sharp tang of vodka. Clearly, whoever mixed this went heavy on the booze. Oh well, it's free, and I'm really hoping it'll help me get through this party. "They aren't, like, eating the psychology majors or anything, are they?"

Gabriel grins from behind his cup. "They're in the backyard playing beer pong with some people. Kade's pissed because he's no good at it, and Lex is having the time of his life beating Kade."

Atlas sighs, but I think I almost catch a ghost of a smile on his lips for a second.

"Callaaaaaaa!"

I move around Atlas and find Brighton swaying her hips,

dancing through the growing crowd in the hallway to get to us. She throws her arms around me, and her drink slops over the side of her cup, splashing a bit on the hardwood floor at our feet.

"Damn, Bri. Did you drink an entire keg already?" I tease as she pulls back. Her hazel eyes pop with bright green sparkly eyeshadow that has left bits of glitter across her cheekbones, and she smells of her favorite Chanel perfume and hairspray. The black cocktail dress she's wearing is a second skin, but it looks freaking hot on her.

"I'm so glad you're here," she shouts over the music, smacking a kiss to my cheek and, I'm sure, leaving a bright red lipstick stain behind. "Jason was supposed to meet me here, but I'm pretty sure he's bailing. Something about a big test next week." She waves her free hand around as if she doesn't really care why he's not here, just that he isn't. "Whatever. It doesn't—" Her eyes land on Atlas and her lips break into a wide grin. "Hello again, handsome."

He nods at her. "Brighton. Nice to see you again."

Brighton glances back at me and arches a brow as if asking, *what's his deal?*

I take a gulp of my drink, cringing a bit as the vodka burns all the way to my stomach.

Gabriel steps up beside Atlas and offers Brighton a kind smile, his eyes twinkling with warmth. Ugh, I hate how effortlessly charismatic he is.

"Oh, hello," she says, her gaze flicking between the guys. "Another friend of yours, Cal?"

"I'm Gabriel," he says, "It's nice to meet you, Brighton."

Her eyes widen. "Shit, girl," she says to me, as if the guys can't hear her.

I press my lips together. "Gabriel is a friend, yes," I finally answer.

She turns her attention back to Gabriel. "Well, any friend

of Calla's is a friend of mine." She sticks out her hand, and Gabriel takes it, shaking gently.

The music in the other room changes, and Brighton cheers, spilling her drink again as she grabs my wrist and drags me into the thick of hot, writhing bodies who have turned the living room into a dance floor. It's dark and hazy from sweat and smoke and smells heavily of too many types of cologne and alcohol—and definitely body odor.

I finish the rest of my drink while dancing to a few songs, and Brighton disappears to refill our cups. Another handful of songs, and I've finished another drink, the second one even stronger than the first. Feeling a little more at ease, my hips move smoothly to the beat. I close my eyes and lose myself in the music and warmth of being surrounded by so many people. It allows me to forget who I am, which these days, is a blessing.

My heart rate kicks up when a hand touches my hip, and I spin around expecting a familiar face, but stare in surprise when I find myself looking into the eyes of a stranger.

The guy has black hair, cropped close to his face, bushy eyebrows, and vibrant green eyes. He flashes me a warm smile and leans in to speak in my ear over the music. "I'm Wyatt," he says.

I return the smile, still swaying my hips in time with the song blaring through the room. "Calla." I catch Brighton's grin over Wyatt's shoulder before she wiggles her fingers at me and disappears into the crowd.

He nods, dancing closer, and I get a whiff of tequila and cheap drugstore body spray. "It's nice to meet you, Calla."

"Yeah, you too." I have to shout as the song gets louder going into the chorus.

Wyatt steps in and hesitates before placing his hands on my hips as we move together to the music. I lift my arms and drape them over his shoulders, careful not to spill any of my drink on him, and smile at the way his cheeks flush when I move closer.

"You go to Georgetown?" I ask him, taking another drink from my cup.

He nods, adjusting his grip on my hips. "Third-year economics."

We lean in each time the other speaks, and I find myself enjoying his company.

"That sounds—" My voice cuts off the moment my gaze connects with Lex's across the room. His eyes are wild, filled with silver fire, and my stomach drops. *Shit*. This isn't going to go over well.

Before I can send Wyatt away, Lex parts the crowd and appears to my right.

"Lex—"

"Hands off," he growls at Wyatt, shoving him away from me without hesitation.

Wyatt stumbles back, throwing a confused look my way before scowling at Lex. "What the hell, bro?"

"Bro?" Lex echoes mockingly, his jaw tightening.

A few people glance at us, and panic clamps down on my chest. The last thing I want is to cause a scene.

"Look," Wyatt stammers, "I didn't know she—"

"She's mine," Lex growls. "Now get the fuck out of here."

Shock fills Wyatt's face, and I send him what I hope is an apologetic look before he shakes his head and walks off.

I turn to Lex, down the rest of my drink, and snap, "What the fuck was that?"

His eyes narrow sharply as he steps in, putting us nose-to-nose. "I was going to ask you the same thing."

"I was dancing," I hiss. "You had no right—"

Lex grabs my hips and spins me around, pulling me back against his chest. His lips are at my ear when he says in a deep voice, "You. Are. Ours. Get that through your head."

I try to drive my elbow into his ribs with no success. To anyone looking, it likely appears as if we're dancing closely. "You're insane."

He chuckles, his breath on my neck shooting a shiver down my spine. "I think you like it."

My body heats, and I grit my teeth, wanting to argue that. But I can't, because there's a part of me, no matter how small, that does enjoy it.

I guess I'm a little insane too.

"I thought you were outside with Kade," I grumble, trying to shift the conversation into safer territory.

"Kade is a sore loser. Plus I get bored easily, and humans are annoying."

I roll my eyes. "So you came in here to annoy me." My voice is flat.

The song changes again, and the room erupts in cheers and hollers as more people fill the makeshift dance floor.

"Let me go," I say firmly, "I need a drink."

"Hmm." Lex's lips brush my neck, followed by a gentle, teasing pass of his fangs. "Me too."

I freeze, and my heart slams against my ribcage. I wouldn't put it past Lex to sink his fangs into me in the middle of a room full of witnesses, which is exactly why I say, "Don't you dare."

Lex sucks playfully, his tongue darting out to swirl against my skin, sending heat directly to my core. He knows exactly what he's doing to me as I squirm in his grasp. He leans away just enough to say, "I'm going to let go in a minute, despite knowing that you'd much rather I take you upstairs and fuck you so hard everyone here would be jealous." He nips my earlobe. "You better behave the rest of the evening, or I will start draining these annoying little humans." He turns me around to face him and captures my chin, forcing my gaze to his. "Understand?"

My jaw clenches in his grip, and I narrow my eyes. I have no doubt he'd follow through with that threat, but would the others let him get away with it? I'd like to think not, considering the importance of keeping their existence as vampires discreet, but I really don't know. "Yes," I force out.

"Good girl," he says with a wink. He leans in and presses a kiss to my forehead before dancing through the crowd toward the backyard.

I'm suddenly feeling much too sober. I weave through the crowd of people and grab another drink from the kitchen, sipping on it while I survey the faces around me, some of which I vaguely recognize, but most of which I've never seen before. Finally, I track down Brighton, dancing near the massive but unlit fireplace in the living room.

"Hey!" she hollers, throwing her arm around my shoulder. "I saw you with that super blond dude. You guys were practically fucking over there. What's the deal with that?"

I take a gulp of my drink. "He's..." I trail off, shaking my head, because I have no idea how to explain to Brighton who Lex is. "Just another friend."

She arches a brow at me, setting her empty cup on the wood mantel above the fireplace. "You've had a lot of *friends* show up recently."

"Yeah, I know. They all, um, came here together." I swallow another mouthful of a drink that is definitely way more vodka than it is lemonade.

"Are you going to tell me who they really are?" Brighton asks in between songs, and I falter. She continues, "They watch you like they'll rip anyone limb from limb if they even dare to look at you the wrong way. And blondie scared off that other guy pretty damn quick."

After downing the rest of my drink, I say, "I told you who they are." I can't help the little giggle that slips from my lips.

"Don't worry about them." I glance down at my cup and frown. "I'm empty. You want a refill?"

She nods, grabbing her cup and handing it to me. "Thanks, babe."

"Be right back." I weave back through the crowd as the room seems to tilt and find my way into the kitchen where I fill our cups, leaving enough room so they won't spill while we're dancing.

"Having fun?" Kade's voice in my ear makes me shiver and turn to face him, my cheeks and chest flushed.

"Hmm." I take a drink before setting both cups on a nearby table. "Probably more than you. I heard Lex kicked your ass at beer pong."

He opens his mouth as his eyes narrow, and I can't help the grin that curls my lips. "Bastard," he grumbles under his breath.

I lean up and kiss him softly. He tastes like beer, and the smell of his cologne tickles my nose. "It's okay. We can't all be good at everything."

He peers down at me, curiosity and amusement making his eyes appear lighter. "You're a little drunk, huh?"

I lift my hand and hold my thumb and finger apart to show him *a little bit*. "It was the only way tonight wasn't going to be a complete train wreck."

He shrugs. "We aren't that bad, Calla. Surely, you believe that to some degree."

I frown at him, swallowing another mouthful of hard lemonade. "I don't want to talk about this. So either shut up and dance with me or leave me alone." I grab my drink, down the rest of it, and leave the cup behind, taking Brighton's and heading toward the living room. Kade follows, shaking his head at me, and the smirk on his lips makes my stomach flip flop.

Before I can step into the living room, Kade circles my

waist and pulls me to him, pressing his lips against my hair. "You've got me wrapped around your finger, you know that?"

My pulse spikes, and I set Brighton's drink on the closest surface before wrapping my arms around Kade's neck. I lean up in the same moment he dips his face closer, and our lips crash together. We battle for control—I grip the back of his hair and his hands cup my ass, hauling me against him. His erection presses into my core, and I gasp into his mouth. He breaks the kiss and drags his lips along my jaw. When he reaches my neck, I tilt my head, exposing it to him as my heart pounds. The room falls away, and it's only the two of us and his mouth on me. His fangs scrape slowly across my skin, making the hair at the back of my neck stand straight with anticipation of his bite.

"Kade," I breathe, practically clinging to him.

His tongue darts out, and I hold my breath. The music pounds in my ear, but it feels as if I'm hearing it from underwater. I don't want to be here anymore. I want *him*.

He trails kisses up and across my jaw again until his mouth presses to the corner of mine. "Later," he promises, as if reading my mind.

"*Now*," I push, tightening my grip on him.

"Easy, angel," Gabriel says from behind me.

I pull away from Kade and freeze when my gaze lands on where Atlas is speaking to Brighton across the room. The lemonade suddenly feels heavy in my stomach as I watch Bri's confused expression. She looks alert and, well, not glamoured, but whatever Atlas is saying to her is—

"… Calla."

I shake my head, pulling my gaze away from my best friend and… whatever Atlas is to me. I'll press him later about what he was talking to her about. For now, I turn back to Kade and Gabriel. "Huh?"

"Are you ready to leave?"

I pull my phone out and squint at the bright screen. We've been here for nearly three hours. It passed in a blur of alcohol, dancing, and handsy vampires—and now my head is pounding. "Yeah," I say.

Lex chooses that moment to appear and hands me another cup. "Water," he says with his signature wink. "Drink up. Atlas will kill you if you puke in his car."

I scowl at that but sip on the water anyway.

Gabriel catches Atlas's gaze and nods to him, and the three of us walk around the edge of the room, meeting him in the hallway.

"You're leaving?" Brighton asks, frowning.

Nodding, I hand Lex the water and pull Brighton into a hug. "You want a lift home?"

"Nah, I've still got some party in me." Her eyes roam over to the group of guys waiting for me. Something shifts in her gaze, but I can't put my finger on it before it's gone. "I'll call you tomorrow." With that, she dances back into the crowd.

I finish the water on the way to the car, the cool air making me more aware and less nauseous.

"You good?" Lex checks, his eyes flicking across my face, studying it to see for himself.

I shoot him a sarcastic thumbs-up. "I'm so good."

Kade chuckles from beside me and throws his arm around my shoulders. The gravel crunches under our feet and the dark, crisp air fills with fog with each exhale.

Atlas unlocks the Escalade, and we pile in, him and Gabriel in the front, and me, Lex, and Kade in the back.

I tip my head back against the seat, then end up leaning into Kade. He lifts his hand and pets my hair soothingly, and I close my eyes, humming softly at the sensation of his touch. I slide my hand across my lap until I reach Lex's, then entwine my fingers through his. He traces slow circles on the back of my hand.

"Calla," Lex murmurs.

"Lex," I say back.

"Open your legs."

My pulse ticks faster, and I pry my eyes open to find him staring at me with liquid silver eyes. He wets his lips, and the breath halts in my lungs. The ache between my legs from before announces itself once more, and my chest rises and falls quicker as Kade reaches for one leg while Lex reaches for the other, and the two of them slowly spread them open.

I watch, completely enraptured, as Lex slides his hand under the emerald fabric of my dress. I suck in a sharp breath when his fingers reach the heat between my legs.

He smirks at Kade. "You owe me fifty bucks."

"What the fuck?" My voice is uneven and breathy.

The rumble of Kade's laugher vibrates against my back. "No panties," he whispers in my ear, and I press my lips together.

Lex drags a single digit along my slit, and my legs widen, desperate for his touch. He pulls back, tutting his tongue, and I narrow my eyes at him. His gaze holds mine as he trails his finger along the inside of my right thigh and then my left.

"You're teasing her," Kade says. "Her heart is about to beat out of her chest and attack you."

I nod in agreement, trying to push closer to Lex, but he pulls his hand back just as I manage to get his fingers to brush my mound. "Fuck you," I grumble.

Lex tilts his head, a bit of white hair falling into his face. "Hmm, only if you're a good girl."

My cheeks fill with heat as Kade wraps his arms around my middle, sliding his hands along the front of my dress. I'm hyperaware of every inch of me he's touching. I'm so focused on his hands now, that when Lex plunges his finger into my pussy, I cry out in surprise. The shocked sound quickly turns into one of pleasure as he curls his finger and massages my tight walls.

Kade reaches up and pinches my nipples through my dress, and they stiffen into hard peaks under his ministrations.

Lex thrusts a few times before holding his finger inside my hot tunnel. His thumb grazes my clit, and I jump in the seat, pushing his finger in deeper.

"Holy shit," I gasp.

"You want more?" Lex asks, searching my gaze as he drags his tongue over his bottom lip.

"Yes," I say immediately.

He arches a brow. "Yes, what?"

I narrow my eyes. "Yes *please*."

He smiles. "Good girl."

Kade presses his lips against the side of my neck and I tilt my head to give him better access, biting the inside of my cheek to keep from moaning loudly as Lex adds a second finger and continues thrusting slowly. He circles my clit hard and fast with his thumb, and it doesn't take me long to reach the edge.

I'm panting hard, and when I look up, my eyes meet Gabriel's gaze in the rearview mirror. The lust that darkens his eyes sends me over the edge. I clamp down hard on Lex's fingers and cry out my release, whimpering when Kade's fangs sink into my neck. I ride Lex's fingers, circling my hips as much as I can in the backseat, all the while holding Gabriel's gaze from the front seat.

My head spins, either from the blood Kade is drinking from me, or the intense waves of pleasure crashing through me, I don't really care. I've never felt this way, never knew I *could* feel this way.

Lex pulls his fingers out slowly, and my gaze finally moves away from Gabriel, just in time to watch Lex lick his fingers clean. My eyes widen, and Kade pulls away from my neck, dragging his tongue along the puncture marks to stop them from bleeding.

I steal a glance at Atlas when his growl rumbles through the car. His gaze is focused on the road, but his knuckles are white, holding the steering wheel in a death grip. Smugness fills me at his rigid posture, and my lips curl into a sleepy smile. *He's jealous.*

I yawn, my brain foggy from sensory overload, and fall back against the seat, holding onto both Kade and Lex. Minutes later, my eyes flutter shut, and I feel more content than I have in days.

I'm in some in-between state of sleep and consciousness when we pull into the garage. I slip in and out but am vaguely aware of being carried in Gabriel's arms. The plush warmth of my bed envelopes me a few minutes later, and I slip into the darkness once more.

## 14

The smell of bacon and coffee lures me out of bed and into the kitchen the next day. I peek down at my PJs; someone must've taken off my dress last night, because now I'm wearing a black T-shirt that barely reaches my knees.

There's a glass of orange juice and a bottle of ibuprofen on the counter. I pop a couple and swallow them down with some juice.

"Morning," Gabriel says from the stove where he's flipping the bacon in a sizzling pan.

I lift my hand in a pathetic wave, still not fully awake. I shuffle over to the coffee maker and press a bunch of buttons until, eventually, I end up with an Americano. I sit at the kitchen table, nursing my steaming mug, and stare out at the pool. The water is even, unmoving. There isn't much of a breeze today, but it still looks chilly out.

"How did you sleep?"

"Dead to the world," I reply, sipping the strong coffee and sighing happily as the steam warms my face, making my nose tingle. "Where are the others?"

"Kade and Lex are still asleep, and Atlas is out for a run."

I glance outside again. I could handle a workout. Sweat out the rest of the lethargy clinging to my muscles. "Has he been gone long?"

"About an hour." He flips the bacon onto a plate and sets it on the table. "Eat. You'll feel better."

I lift my mug to my lips. "I'm all set."

He stands in front of me. "Coffee is not food, angel," he says dryly.

I pout. "Let me live my life."

He pushes the bacon closer. "Don't make me tell you again." The authority in his voice has me reaching for a piece of bacon without hesitation.

I take a bite and chew slowly. It tastes freaking amazing, because of course it does. "Thanks, Gabriel." I shoot him a small smile. "You're always looking out for me." I glance at my lap. "I'm assuming you changed my clothes last night?"

He nods when I look back up at him. "You can keep my shirt. I like the way it looks on you."

My smile morphs into a grin. "Good. I was going to keep it anyway. It's super comfy."

The corner of his mouth curls, and he snags a piece of bacon off the plate, biting half of it off. "You like your eggs poached, right?"

I nod, figuring there's no point in arguing about eating breakfast. "You don't need to cook for me, though. I can make, well, not much, but still."

He chews the other half of his piece of bacon and swallows. "I enjoy taking care of you."

I blink at him in surprise, taking another sip of my Americano. "I can't imagine when the four of you made that deal with my ancestors that you did so expecting to put me to bed and cook me breakfast."

He pauses, scratching the shadow of stubble at his jaw.

He's usually clean-shaven, but I like this slightly disheveled look on him. "Perhaps not," he says softly. "Regardless, I'm happy to do it."

I decide there's not much else to say. I tried to subtly get some information, and it didn't necessarily backfire like it did the other night, but I'm still no further ahead when it comes to information.

After breakfast, I sneak upstairs and change into bright purple leggings and a matching cropped workout top. I grab a bottle of water on my way to the gym and flick the lights and ceiling fans on when I get inside. I warm up for a few minutes on the treadmill before approaching the heavy punching bag hanging from a thick beam across the ceiling. I've never been much into boxing, but the building pressure in my chest tells me it might do me some good to punch something over and over to exert some frustrated energy.

The first time my fist connects with the bag, a grin splits across my lips. *This is fun.* I stick my wireless headphones in and turn the music way up, losing myself in the beat as my body moves instinctively, punching and kicking the bag until my chest is heaving with shallow breaths and my heart is pounding so hard it feels moments away from breaking free from my ribcage.

I turn to grab my water bottle off the floor and yelp when I find Atlas leaning against the wall, watching me. I rip my headphones out as I struggle to catch my breath. "What... are you... doing?"

"Your form is pathetic," he says, pushing away from the wall and walking closer.

I drop my headphones next to my water bottle and cross my arms. "Gee, thanks for the unsolicited critique."

He stops a few feet away, his jaw tight. When he opens his mouth to speak, his fangs are extended. "You're bleeding."

The color drains from my face, and I step back, only to hit the punching bag. I glance down at my hands and see that my knuckles are an angry red, raw and throbbing with pain. My left knuckle is split open in one place, which is where the blood is coming from. I didn't feel it until now. I cover the injury with my other hand and press my lips together.

Atlas swallows visibly, not moving an inch as he keeps his eyes on me. His fangs retract after a tense moment, and he seems to relax a little. "I'm sorry. I haven't had an opportunity to feed in a couple of days."

I nod, because what else am I supposed to do?

He steps closer again, effectively swallowing what little distance I'd been able to put between us. Without a word, he picks up my injured hand, cradling my wrist gently.

"It's fine," I mumble.

"I can heal it," he says in a low voice, his fangs extending again.

I stiffen and try to pull my hand back, but he holds it tighter. "I—"

"Relax, Calla. I'm not going to hurt you. You're doing a good enough job of that yourself."

"I'll just wrap it up. It's fine," I repeat, my pulse racing beneath my skin; surely he can feel it against his palm.

"You live with four vampires who all want a taste of you. Are you sure that's what you want to do?"

I chew the inside of my cheek. "F-fine."

Atlas nods, then lifts his other hand to his mouth. He quickly bites into the skin of his palm, and dark red blood pools in his hand. "Drink," he says.

Panic seizes me, and I try to pull away again. I have no idea what I thought he was going to do to heal me, but I wasn't prepared for *this*.

"Calla—"

"No," I croak, my heart pounding in my ears. "I can't. That's not... No."

He sighs. "It will heal your injury."

My voice shakes when I say, "I'm telling you, I can't." I'm not trying to be difficult, but the thought of drinking his blood has sweat dotting my brow and my heart beating quicker than it should.

"Let me help you?" His voice is softer than I've heard it before. It makes me pause. Do I trust him? Hell to the no, but there's also something telling me he's being decent here, and I should let him.

"Okay," I finally say, cringing at how weak my voice comes out.

His grip on my wrist softens, and he traces his thumb back and forth across my skin. When he speaks again, his voice is a warm caress that I instantly get lost in. "You're going to drink from me, and it's going to make you better. You don't need to panic or be ashamed. Allow yourself to enjoy it." He leans down so his lips are close to my ear. "Drink, Calla."

I move without hesitation, cradling his hand in my less injured one. I bring it to my lips, and he tips it back. Copper warmth pours into my mouth and explodes across my tastebuds. My eyes close on their own, and I step in closer, closing my lips around the puncture marks in his hand. I swallow greedily, shocked at how electrifying the sensation of drinking blood is. Energy zips through me, and I open my eyes as I pull back, sucking in a short breath. My eyes drop to where Atlas is holding onto my hand, and I gape at the sight of completely healed skin. It's not even tinged red. It's as if it hadn't happened at all.

"Holy shit," I breathe.

He lets go and steps back, watching me closely. "Take a

minute. Vampire blood can be overwhelming for humans, especially that of a born immortal."

I squint at him, the light above us suddenly much brighter than it was a few minutes ago. The buzz of electricity echoes in my ears. "A born immortal?"

"As opposed to a turned one," he explains. "The others were turned. I, however, was born a vampire."

Right. I knew that. "Is that why you can glamour people differently?"

"Yes."

"What else makes you different?"

He arches a brow. "Not much else, really. I'm faster and stronger, harder to kill, and don't need human food to survive. But you already knew that part."

I nod, cringing when a wave of dizziness rushes over me, and I sway, reaching out blindly.

Atlas catches me, steadying me in his arms. "Easy," he murmurs.

My cheek presses against the soft fabric of his shirt, and I glance up at him. There's a brief moment where I think I see concern in his silver gaze, but it's gone as quick as it came. "Thank you," I whisper.

"You're welcome."

The room has stopped spinning, but I don't move away. Being close to him like this makes me feel... powerful. I don't know what it is. Maybe it's his blood running through my veins, but I feel connected to him in a way that I haven't been with the others.

"Tell me," I blurt.

His dark brows knit as he peers down at me. "Tell you what?"

I lick the dryness from my lips, then press them together for a moment before saying, "What you're going to do with me."

He exhales a deep breath, stirring the hair at my temple. "Calla…" There's a warning in his voice.

"Please." I put as much force into that one word as I can. "Atlas, I can't stand living with not knowing. If you're going to kill me, just please—"

He cups my cheeks, tilting my head back so I'm looking into his eyes. "Slow down. Breathe. No one is going to hurt you. Killing you would be pointless. A waste of an asset."

My stomach sinks. Maybe I should be relieved by that, but there's a part of me that is hurt by his words. Not to mention being wildly confused by them, considering I have no idea what I could possibly do for them that would make me an asset, especially when they won't tell me a fucking thing. Living in the dark is chipping away at my sanity.

I huff out a sigh. "What would you do in my position? Would you just accept being kept in the dark and given scraps of pretty useless information every now and then?" When he opens his mouth to respond, I keep talking. "I mean, what's the point, Atlas? Really? Be honest with me, please. If I'm just a human plaything for the lot of you, at least let me know. I'm grateful you've had the decency to let me continue my studies—mostly because it gives me something to do that isn't sitting around here wondering what's going to happen tomorrow, but—"

My words are cut off when the sound of shouting from inside the house reaches us. Atlas's brows furrow and his jaw tightens, making my stomach churn nervously.

The shouting gets louder. There are at least three different voices, all sharp and filled with venom, but I can't hear exact words, just noise.

I frown at Atlas. "What's going on?"

"Nothing you need to worry about," he says without looking my way.

Frustration overpowers my nerves, and I take a couple of steps toward the door to the garage that will take me into the house. "Fine, then I guess I'll go see for myself."

His eyes flash with anger, and he moves in a blur of darkness, appearing in front of me in the space of a heartbeat. "The hell you will." He's a solid wall of muscle and supernatural strength, but I refuse to back down.

"Move," I snap at him.

He merely arches a brow.

I scowl. "Atlas, *move*."

"Make me," he taunts, knowing full well that isn't possible. Bastard.

My eyes narrow sharply as the shouting inside continues, and I cross my arms. "I'm fucking sick of the secrets."

"I don't give a shit, Calla. You're not going in there."

"You can't just—"

A door slams, making the house shake from the force, and I jump, my heart leaping into my throat. The shouting has stopped and the house is eerily silent.

"Fine," he says, "go ahead."

I glare at him and storm away, jogging down the stairs and through the garage into the house. By the time I close the door behind me, it's only Lex and Gabriel in the living room, talking in hushed voices. They glance over at me when I walk in, and Gabriel smiles warmly, as if whatever just had them shouting didn't happen.

"Will someone please explain what just happened? Because—"

The garage door opens, and Atlas struts in, his expression dark as he looks between the others. He heard the conversation that happened before I came in.

"Because he won't tell me a damn thing," I finish, jerking my thumb back at Atlas.

Lex smirks. "Nothing we can't handle, which means you don't need to worry about it."

Pressure builds in my chest, and I clench my jaw hard. The desire to scream rips through me, and Gabriel must see that on my face because he catches my attention and nods, offering me a look that says, *I understand your frustration*. His gaze drops to my hands, and he frowns. "You were bleeding."

Shit. I quickly wipe my hands on my leggings. "I'm fine," I assure him. *Physically, at least*, I fight the urge to add.

"Go take a shower," Atlas says in a low voice from beside me. "All any of us can smell is your blood."

My throat goes dry, and I flick a subtle glance between Lex and Gabriel. "Sorry," I mumble.

Lex's responding laugh is a deep, rich sound that booms through the room. "You don't need to apologize for bleeding, you silly little human. We are capable of controlling ourselves."

"Speak for yourself," Kade says, walking into the room. His silver eyes are dark with hunger and something else, and I shift away from him.

I swallow hard. "Tell me what's going on, then I'll take a damn shower."

Lex seems highly amused by my ultimatum, still smirking as he perches on the arm of the couch. Gabriel stands next to him and sighs, shifting his attention to Atlas.

"We can talk about it later," Atlas says.

"Bullshit," I snap. I'm not leaving this room until I get *something*.

His brows lift, and he crosses his arms over his chest. Thick cords of vein pop when he flexes his arms, and I hate that I notice that before forcing myself to look back at his face. Which, let's face it, is just as nice to look at. *Fuck me.*

"Calla—" Gabriel starts.

"No," I cut him off in a sharp tone. "I'm not going

anywhere until you..." My voice trails off as I catch movement out of my peripheral.

Kade walks toward me at a normal pace, and my brows pinch together as he gets closer. I retreat a step, only to have my back collide with Atlas's chest.

"What—"

Kade smirks. "You're getting in the shower whether you like it or not. I'll throw you over my shoulder if you don't care to walk there yourself."

Atlas gives me a push toward Kade, and in the time it takes me to blink, he has me over his shoulder.

"What the fuck," I holler. "Let me down!"

He slaps my ass, and I yelp in surprise. Beating my fists into his back as he walks through the house to the bathroom connected to the room I've been sleeping in, my breathing quickly becomes labored.

"You need to settle down," he says, his voice filled with amusement. The motherfucker is enjoying this.

I try kicking him, but it does nothing. "Kade, I swear to god, if you don't—"

He sets me on the marble floor, but before I can move, he pins me to the wall beside the doorway, his fingers wrapped around my throat, firm but not so tight I can't breathe. "Keep talking," he warns, flashing his fangs, "and I'll fuck you against this wall until you can't speak."

All the words in my vocabulary are suddenly gone. I stare at him, my heart pounding against my chest so hard I can feel it in my ears. Heat rises in my cheeks and pools low in my belly.

Kade's lips curl into a slow smirk. "Though that might be exactly what you want." He tilts his head, looking into my eyes. "Is that what you want, Calla?"

My lips part, but I don't speak—I can't. Instead, I shake my head. *I'm a fucking liar.*

He leans in, taking up my entire world. "Deny it all you want." His nose grazes mine, and he braces his free hand on the wall beside my head. "Your body won't lie about what it craves."

Kade's lips crash down on mine, and I moan into his mouth, succumbing to everything I hate.

## 15

Kade lifts me, and I instinctively wrap my legs around his waist as we move toward the shower. His lips are soft against mine, and he kisses me slowly, coaxing my mouth open so he can slide his tongue in and graze mine. He manages to turn on the shower without breaking the kiss or dropping me, and the bathroom fills with steam as we lose ourselves in each other.

I pull back enough to take a breath and say, "I don't know about you, but I don't usually shower clothed."

He smirks, leaning back in to place a chaste kiss against my mouth. "No?" He sets me down and tugs his shirt off over his head in a quick motion, dropping it in a pile on the floor. Not a minute later, his bottoms join it, leaving him completely bared to me.

I can't stop my eyes from wandering. From his broad chest and chiseled abs to the long, thick—

"My face is up here," he says in a dry tone.

I lift my gaze, but surprisingly, I'm not embarrassed. I was openly gawking at him, because yeah, he's sexy as hell. He knows it too. I lick my lips, pressing them together. The room is becoming hazier by the minute, and warmth clings to my skin.

Kade steps closer. "Lift your arms." When I comply, he peels my sports bra off over my head, adding it to the pile of his clothes. When his eyes fall to my breasts, I move to cover myself, but he easily catches my wrists and holds me open to him. "Don't hide from me," he says in a smooth voice.

I chew my bottom lip as my cheeks burn, and Kade lifts my arms, draping them over his shoulders before dipping his face and sealing his mouth over mine in a feverish kiss that has my head spinning in a matter of seconds. My breasts press against his bare chest, and the friction makes my nipples stiffen into hard peaks, begging to be touched. I moan into his mouth, and he grips my hips, tugging me harder against him. The heat between my legs pulses, and I break the kiss to pull off my leggings, leaving us both naked and devouring each other with our eyes.

Kade backs me up until I'm standing under the hot spray of water, and I close my eyes when he grips my chin, tilting my head back to kiss me again. My lips move against his, and I trail my fingers up the tight muscles of his stomach as the water cascades down on us. He uses his other hand to palm my breast, pinching my nipple and making me gasp against his lips. I arch my back, pushing my breast into his hand as I kiss him harder. He forces his tongue into my mouth in the same moment his hand switches sides, delivering the same delicious ministrations to my other breast. My pulse kicks up when he presses his lower half into me, his hard shaft brushing the sensitive skin between my legs. I've never ached for someone like this. The tension building is almost painful in its intensity.

I nip at his lower lip, and he groans in response, pulling back for a short moment before burying his face in the crook of my neck. His lips trail along my skin, and when his fangs extend and scrape across the spot where my shoulder meets my neck, my breath catches. I'm not sure what I want more—for him to fuck me or bite me. If I'm honest with myself, I want both—preferably at the same time.

Kade's fingers trail down my stomach, making my skin tingle, and stops just shy of my entrance. My breathing quickens in anticipation, but he doesn't move. Hours pass, or maybe it's only seconds.

"Kade..." My voice is gravelly, filled with lust, and it only makes my heart beat faster.

"Hmm?" His tongue darts out and swirls against my skin.

"Do *something*," I practically growl.

He pulls back and meets my gaze. "Tell me what you want."

My lips part before I snap my mouth shut. Finally, I say, "You know what I want."

Kade nods. "I want to hear you say it."

I narrow my eyes at him as water drips from his hair down his face. "Fuck. Me."

He smirks, pressing one hand against the shower wall as he leans in. "Come on, Calla. You can do better than that." He grips his thick length in his fist and teases my opening, dragging the tip of his cock along my slit. He lowers his voice and speaks into my ear. "Use your words and tell me exactly what you want me to do to you." He leans back, flicking his tongue along his bottom lip.

I nod, tipping my head back against the shower tile and holding his gaze. "I... I want you to pin me against this wall and drive your cock inside me." His eyes are liquid silver as I continue, my heart hammering in my chest. "I want you... to fuck me so hard I can't hold myself up, and right before I'm about to collapse... I want you to sink your fangs into my neck and drink from me while I come around your cock."

Kade stiffens against my entrance. "Fucking hell," he growls.

"Is that descriptive enough for you?" I ask, tilting my head.

His eyes are dark and hooded as he pushes his tip inside me half an inch. "Yes, Calla," he says in a low voice, slowly moving in deeper.

I press my lips together, my eyes flicking between his as my breath halts. I grit my teeth at the discomfort, my body not accustomed to someone so large.

"You need to relax," Kade says, holding himself barely inside of me. The muscles in his arms are tight; he's holding himself back from driving into me.

I struggle to find my voice as I widen my stance a bit. "I'm trying." I take a deep breath, and the tension in my lower body eases slightly. "Keep going," I tell him.

He pushes in a little more and reaches between us, circling my clit with his thumb. "You're so fucking tight," he says, leaning in and pressing his forehead to mine. "I love it."

At his words, a rush of warmth spreads through me, and I arch my back, pushing him in deeper.

"There we go," he murmurs, peppering kisses along my jaw, "just a little more."

He stands still, letting me move at my own pace, spearing myself on his cock until, eventually, he's completely inside me. He gives me a minute to adjust, playing lazily with my clit until my breathing quickens, then he pulls out almost all the way before thrusting back in, stealing my breath.

"Holy shit," I gasp.

Kade grins. "I'll take that as a compliment."

I roll my eyes. "Even when you're fucking me, you are insufferable."

He thrusts harder, a challenging glint in his eyes.

Clenching around him, I grab the back of his neck and

pull him to me, sealing my mouth over his. At least if we're kissing, he can't ruin this by talking. Our mouths move together as Kade thrusts into me, deep and slow, and then faster. He brings me to the edge several times, easing off just as the delicious pressure builds to new heights.

I growl against his lips, meeting his thrusts, but he shoves me back against the shower wall and holds me there so I can't move my hips, and continues his languid pace.

His mouth moves from my lips to my neck, kissing and sucking playfully. "Do you want to come?" he murmurs, tracing the shell of my ear with his lips.

My pulse spikes as he holds himself still inside me. "Yes," I ground out.

He rolls his hips, pushing in deeper and hitting a particularly sensitive spot. "Yes, what?"

"What, you're going to make me beg for it now?"

"Hmm, no. But you would if I asked, and we both know it." He thrusts hard and fast, making me gasp in surprise. I hold onto his shoulders to keep myself upright, and my moans fill the steamy room as he pounds into me over and over. The tension builds, and when Kade finds my clit with his fingers, I come undone. I clench around him in the same moment he sinks his fangs into my neck, drinking deeply as he continues thrusting into me.

I cry out, and he catches me when my legs give out. His cock pulses inside me, and my skin tingles with pleasure. I keep my eyes closed as I catch my breath, only opening them when he pulls out of me and backs us into the stream of water. He pulls away from my neck and lets the water wash away the blood before he sets me on the stone bench on the other side of the shower. I'm eye level with his cock, and when I reach for it, he turns to the side and captures my chin between his fingers, tilting my head back so I'm looking at his face.

"But you didn't—"

"That wasn't about me." His eyes take a quick scan of my body. "Can you stand?" He releases my chin and holds his hands out to me.

I take them, allowing him to help me get up. He kisses me softly, slowly, and then he reaches behind me for the shampoo bottle. I'm a little stunned, so when he squirts shampoo onto his hand and turns me around to start washing my hair, I say nothing. I let Kade take care of me, and it's... really fucking nice.

***

The five of us sit down for dinner, and the kitchen is filled with the savory aroma of roast and potatoes—one of my favorite meals. It's no coincidence, I'm sure. These guys did their homework.

I sit beside Atlas, with Kade and Lex across from me and Gabriel at the head of the table. Reaching for the water pitcher, I meet Gabriel's gaze and say, "Are we going to talk about what happened earlier, or what?" I pour myself some water before returning the pitcher to its spot in the middle of the table. When Gabriel doesn't answer and instead glances toward Atlas, my gaze follows. Everything seems to lead to Atlas. I watch his reaction, but his expression is, as always, infuriatingly impassive.

He sighs audibly and glances around the table at the rest of the guys before settling his gaze on me. His eyes are dark and his jaw is set tight. The nerves in my stomach are knots of unease with little flickers of excitement, because despite the tension hanging in the air, it seems as if I'm *finally* going to get some answers. It's about damn time.

"Calla," Gabriel says, pulling my attention away from

Atlas. "There's a vampire in New York who is looking for you."

I blink at him, then shake my head. Clearly I misheard him, because that makes no sense. "I don't understand," I say in a quiet voice. The nerves in my stomach have turned to concrete.

He frowns. "There's a lot to it, but we aren't the only vampires your family was associated with years ago. This particular vampire was involved in the business deal we helped your ancestor out of."

"What's that got to do with me? From what I've been told, the oath was only made between my family and the four of you."

"That's right," Atlas says. "There's no merit to Dante's claim to you, but that doesn't eliminate the threat. He wants something to make up for losing out on that deal. He wants your blood in exchange for what he lost. He also has a bone to pick with us for some shit that went down decades ago, but that really isn't what's important here."

*Claim to me?* My eyes widen at the vaguely familiar name, recalling the phone call I'd overheard Atlas on when that name came up. "And this vampire—Dante—he was here earlier?"

"No," Kade cuts in. "That was Marcel. The arguing you heard was the result of the less than ideal information he provided us."

"Marcel?" I ask, my brows knitting.

"He's an informant of ours," Gabriel explains, taking a sip from his glass that is filled with dark red liquid too thick to be wine.

Kade stabs his piece of roast, slicing a piece off and biting it off his fork. "Apparently Dante has been sniffing around a few of our buildings in the city since word spread that we fulfilled the oath." He swallows and adds, "Guess he figured we'd be keeping you there."

Instead of asking any number of other, far more important questions, I say, "You have properties in New York too?" It hardly matters, and I'm not even sure why I asked.

Lex shrugs. "Real estate is a good investment." It's the same thing he told me when I discovered he owned the building I'd been living in.

I nod absently. "So what exactly does this mean?" Part of me is glad they're finally telling me what's going on, but knowing there's a vampire out there looking for me makes me miss the ignorance of being kept in the dark just a little bit. I try to shake the chill that seems to have settled in my bones, but it's not going anywhere. I swallow past the lump in my throat and push a potato around my plate, chewing my bottom lip.

I glance across the table when Lex murmurs my name.

"We're not going to let anything happen to you while you're with us," he says with what I'm sure is meant to be an encouraging wink, but it doesn't help the pressure building in my chest.

I stare at him for a moment. "That's your plan? Guard me twenty-four seven? I have school and a life I built before the four of you came around and screwed it up. This is insane, I —" I push away from the table and stand. "I didn't sign up for any of this." I blink back the sudden urge to cry. From fear or frustration—or a combination of both—I'm not entirely sure.

Atlas touches my arm, and my world narrows on him. "Sit down," he says in a silky voice.

My body complies while my mind screams profanities at being overpowered by vampiric glamour. I scowl when he pulls his hand back. "I'm allowed to be upset."

"Of course you are," Atlas agrees. "What you're not allowed to do is run away from us."

"Certainly not before hearing our kick-ass plan to ensure your safety," Lex says focusing on his plate as he drowns his roast in gravy, as if we're not talking about how to protect me from an immortal who wants me dead because my family was the reason—at least in part—that he didn't get what he wanted all those years ago.

I take a deep breath, exhaling a heavy sigh. "Okay, fine." I glance around the table. "What's your brilliant idea?"

## 16

It's been two weeks since I found out about the vampire named Dante who wants to kill me.

According to the guys, they've sent Dante on a wild-goose chase looking for me. I suppose it helps that they have property all over the United States—but it's only a matter of time before Dante comes to Washington.

"You're distracted today."

I blink until Atlas's face comes into focus. His silver eyes are tired, and he hasn't shaved in enough days that he's grown a bit of a beard. I don't hate it, I decide as I stare at it for a moment. "Sorry," I mumble, lifting my arms into the defensive stance we've been practicing over the last week. Since finding out about Dante, I've been adamant about training daily again despite what Lex said about me being safe while I'm with them. Evidently all I needed to reignite the fire in me to protect myself against the supernatural was a threat against my life by one of them. "I'm good."

"I could have killed you a dozen different ways in the time you were spacing out," he says flatly.

I roll my eyes. "You sure know how to cheer a girl up, Atlas. Has anyone ever told you that?"

His expression doesn't change. "No."

"Shocking," I mutter dryly.

He cocks his head to the side. "You want to keep running your mouth at me, or do you want to train?"

I prop my hands on my hips. "Hmm... Option C, all of the above?"

Atlas shrugs. "If you're prepared to defend yourself with witty comebacks, I won't waste my time with you in here." He turns his back on me, heading for the door.

I grit my teeth. "Wait."

He keeps walking.

"Atlas!"

He stops, keeping his back to me.

I storm over to him, and right as I'm about to launch into a maneuver *he* taught me, he turns, causing me to collide with his solid chest.

"Sloppy," he chastises, steadying me. Instead of letting go, he hauls me against him.

I grip his forearms, my mouth suddenly dry. "Wh-what are you doing?"

He leans down until our lips are barely an inch apart. "Fight me off."

Excitement swirls in my stomach and heat gathers south of there. I lick the dryness from my lips and take a steadying breath. "How do you suggest I do that?" I ask in a low voice, hyperaware of the race in my pulse.

"I don't care how, Calla. Figure it out."

I frown. "Anything I do, you'll see it coming. Any maneuver will be too slow to be effective and certainly won't be strong enough."

He nods. "Do it anyway. You might surprise yourself—or

your opponent, which is the important part. It will buy you time to run, which is why you've been doing that every day too. The faster and longer you can run, the better chance you have at—"

"Not having my throat ripped out? Yeah, I got that."

His grip on my hips tightens as a muscle feathers along his jaw. "That's not going to happen."

I tilt my head, searching his face for *anything*. "Would that upset you?" I ask.

Atlas blinks at me. "What?"

"My death," I say simply.

He narrows his eyes ever so slightly, barely enough to notice. But I do. "You're not going to die."

"First off, that's incorrect. I'm human—I will die. And second, that's not what I asked you."

He pushes me backward, keeping his grip on me, and my back hits the wall. "What would you like to hear me say, Calla?" he says in a low voice.

I swallow hard, forcing myself to hold his intense gaze. "I want you to answer my question. It's not a hard one."

His jaw works as his eyes dance across my face. "I don't wish to see you dead, no."

I press my lips together against a smile despite the restless beat of my heart in my chest. "Now how hard was that?"

Atlas drags one hand up my side, his fingers skimming over my arm and leaving goose bumps in their wake. He wraps his fingers around the side of my neck, using his thumb under my chin to tilt my head back against the wall. His gaze makes me freeze. Despite what he just said, I can't tell if he's about to kiss me or tear into my throat himself.

"Tell me to walk away," he says gruffly, the space between his brows creased with tension.

I reach for him, sliding my hands up his chest. "No." My voice is soft, barely above a whisper.

Surprise flickers across his features. "Calla—"

"I don't want you to leave," I tell him. "I want you to kiss me." Things with Atlas are noticeably different than with the others. More intense in a way I couldn't have expected. But I crave him nonetheless. I could continue denying it, but that hasn't gotten me anywhere thus far, so what's the point?

His thumb moves slowly along my jaw. "This is a dangerous path we're heading down," he warns, but he doesn't move away.

"Nothing about my life is safe these days," I offer. "It never was."

He shakes his head. "This is different."

"How?" I push.

"Because of *you*," he says. "You're human."

"And you're a vampire," I say plainly. "Now that we've cleared that up—"

"I don't want to rip you apart," he snaps. "Before when I said you wouldn't survive the things I want to do to you, that wasn't a lie, Calla."

I stand there silently, because what the hell am I supposed to say to that? Should I admit that I'm curious, that an incredibly reckless part of me wants to try it—whatever *it* is—anyway? Yeah, probably not.

"Don't," he warns, clearly seeing something on my face that gave away my thoughts.

I pull his hand away from my face and hold it between both of mine. "You're not going to break me."

He laughs darkly on a harsh exhale. "You have no idea what I could do to you."

"You're right, I don't. But you're not going to scare me away. You're stuck with me as much as I'm stuck with you, so we may as well make the best of it."

"You have three other guys walking around this house who are more than willing to see to whatever you need and desire."

I nod. "And they do so quite well. But I want *you*."

Atlas pulls his hand free and slams it against the wall next to my head. "You're playing with fire." His voice makes me shiver and his grip on my hip tightens, warming my skin through my joggers.

"Then burn me," I breathe, grabbing the front of his shirt and tugging him to me.

His nose grazes mine, and the moment his lips brush mine, my eyes flutter shut, and I melt into him. He kisses me painfully slow, his entire body tense with restraint.

I slide my hands up his chest and wrap them around his neck. "Relax," I murmur against his lips. I'm surprised when he actually does, leaning into me and deepening the kiss as his tongue flicks out and traces my lips. My heart thumps loudly in my chest, and I lose myself in the kiss. So much so, that I don't hear the bounding footsteps up the stairs from the garage.

Atlas pulls away from me, and over his shoulder, I see Lex come toward us. I'm expecting some lewd comment about him walking in on us, so when he says nothing, I know something's up.

"Calla, go back to the house," Atlas says.

I whirl on him. "I want to know what's going on."

"And if you need to know, you will," he says pointedly. "Now go back to the house."

"I… Fine." I walk across the room, passing Lex without a word, and jog down the stairs into the garage. The concrete space is cold, making me shiver as I let myself into the house, where Kade and Gabriel are sitting in the living room.

Gabriel glances up from his phone when I close the door behind me, then stands, offering me a warm smile. "Can I make you something for lunch?"

I shake my head. "You can tell me what's going on, though. Lex came upstairs to talk to Atlas, and I got sent in here." I thought I was making progress when it came to being kept in the dark, but the universe is apparently set on proving me wrong.

"They have some things to figure out," Kade says from where he's lounging on the couch, scrolling on his phone. He seems far less concerned than Lex, but it doesn't make me feel better.

"Does this have something to do with that vampire from New York?" My stomach drops as the panic that's been living in my chest for too long now spikes, making my pulse race. "Does he know I'm here?"

Gabriel closes the distance between us in a blur of movement and cups my face in his hands. His grip is warm and gentle. "Take a breath, angel. You're safe. Dante doesn't know where you are."

"He doesn't?" I hate how weak my voice sounds.

Gabriel shakes his head. "What's going on has nothing to do with him. You don't need to worry about it." His eyes shift between mine. "Okay? You have my word." He lets his hands fall back to his sides, but his gaze remains locked with mine.

"Okay," I finally say. "But if Dante is still looking for me, do you think he'll go after my parents?" Despite the strained relationship I've had with them over the years, the thought of them being in danger because of what happened long before I was born—even though that's the very position I'm in—makes my chest feel suffocatingly tight.

"Your parents are safe," Kade says, setting his phone on the coffee table and swinging his legs over the side of the couch as he moves into a sitting position. "Dante is interested in you—and fucking with us—he doesn't care about your mom and dad. He knows you're not with them and, if he's done his research, he likely figures using them to get to you wouldn't be very effective."

He would be wrong about that. They're still my parents. If

they were in danger, I would do whatever was necessary to ensure their safety.

Nausea rolls through me like a vicious, unforgiving wave. I feel like a pawn now more than ever, and that makes me want to scream. I swallow the lump in my throat and straighten my shoulders, holding my chin up.

The garage door opens, and Atlas and Lex walk inside. Lex comes over to me, his expression less severe than it was when he interrupted us in the gym, and slings his arm around my shoulders. He leans in pressing a kiss to the side of my head.

"I should take a shower," I announce. I don't really need to —I didn't get much of a chance to work up a sweat in the gym—but it's a good excuse to get out of this room.

Lex lets me go, and I feel the guys' eyes on me as I walk out of the room. My head is spinning by the time I get to the bedroom and lock the door. I fall back against it, closing my eyes and pressing a hand to my forehead.

I've been here for almost a month now. While I'm not immediately terrified for my life when it comes to the four vampires in the other room, there's still something in my gut that tells me I can't entirely trust them. There's still so much I don't know, so many secrets that are being kept from me for god knows what reason. And despite knowing in my heart that there's no chance I'm getting out of this, there's still a part of me that wants to run, to choose my own fate for once.

I stand in the shower long after I've washed my hair and body, letting the hot water mix with the silent, frustrated tears rolling down my cheeks.

I'm so far out of my element now, I don't even remember what it feels like to have control.

## 17

When I return to the living room after changing into a hoodie and leggings, I frown at the empty room. The sun is shining through the floor-to-ceiling windows, but the wind is hollowing through the trees outside. Mother Nature is as restless as I am today, it seems.

I stand at the window with my arms wrapped around myself, watching the branches sway and drop leaves into the pool.

The sound of the coffee maker catches my attention, and I glance toward the kitchen to find Kade leaning against the counter watching me.

"Where did everyone go?" I ask, walking into the kitchen.

"Lex and Atlas left while you were in the shower." He hands me a steaming cup of coffee, and I take it, wrapping my fingers around the warmth.

"Thanks," I murmur, taking a small sip. "Where did they go?"

He grabs another mug from the cupboard above his head

and sets it under the spout of the coffee maker. "They'll explain when they return."

I set my coffee on the counter. "Or you could just tell me now." There's an edge to my voice that isn't lost on Kade.

His expression is serious when he turns back to me. "I could," he says, "but I'm not going to."

My jaw clenches. "Why not?" I push. "Does this have something to do with Dante?" Gabriel has said it didn't, but that seems unlikely now that Atlas and Lex have taken off. "I deserve to know if something—"

"It has nothing to do with that," he cuts me off, removing his mug from the machine and adding an obscene amount of sugar and a splash of cream. "We're monitoring that situation, and once there's something to know, you'll know it."

"Fine," I huff out, tracing the rim of my mug with my finger. "Then what's this about?"

"Atlas will explain when he returns," Kade repeats.

I narrow my eyes. "And when will that be?"

He shrugs. "Tomorrow maybe."

"Maybe?" I echo, shaking my head and prompting him to offer a more certain answer.

"Hmm." He takes a sip of his coffee. "Don't you have homework or something you should be doing?"

My brows raise. "What are you, my dad?"

He smirks. "Didn't realize you had a daddy kink, Calla. Good to know."

Heat flares in my cheeks. "I don't," I rush to say.

"Hey, I'm not judging. There's no shame in it. A lot of people with strained parental relationships later experience—"

"Please stop talking." I close my eyes, pressing my fingers against my temples in an attempt to ease the tension there.

Kade chuckles. "Lighten up, Calla. I'm just teasing." He reaches over and taps the tip of my nose with his finger. I attempt to bat his hand away, but it's already back at his side before I can catch it. *Stupid vampire speed.*

※

The next morning, Lex and Atlas haven't returned.

I get ready for class as normal despite the pit in my stomach and meet Brighton for brunch at our regular spot. Kade doesn't accompany me to class but assured me before I left the house that I was safe, that they have people looking out for me.

I sit at the back of the lecture hall and try to focus, but I'm finding it increasingly difficult to see the importance of this class when my life seems more and more like a rollercoaster I'll never be able to get off.

Gabriel has gone to work when I return to the house later in the afternoon. I wander around until I find myself standing in Kade's doorway. He's laying on top of the black sheets on his massive bed, his head near the end, with his eyes closed. His expression is soft, peaceful. I can't stop looking at him like this. The sight of him so relaxed eases the tension in my chest ever so slightly. If he's not concerned about everything going on, that should make me feel better, right?

"Are you going to continue to stand there staring at me, or would you like to come in?" he asks without looking my way or even opening his eyes.

I chew my bottom lip, stepping into his bedroom after a moment of hesitation. Glancing around, surprise flickers through me, though I'm not sure why. I guess I didn't expect his room to be so... neat and tidy? Kade has always given off a bit of chaotic energy, so I kind of figured his personal space would reflect that. But nope, the walls are a neutral taupe with long, dark curtains covering the windows across the room. There are small round tables on either side of the bed with matching, exposed bulb lamps. On the other side of the room, twin doors lead to what I imagine are a bathroom and closet, and that's the extent of Kade's bedroom. No art on the walls or decor around the room. It's... I don't know, a little sad? It makes me want to drag his ass to Target and spruce the space up.

"Everything okay?" I ask, slowly approaching the bed.

His chest rises and falls deeply as he exhales a heavy breath. "Just peachy. How was class?"

I press my lips together. "Dull compared to some I've been to."

While his eyes remain closed, his lips twist into a smirk. "I bet."

I walk closer, stopping a few feet from his bed as he opens his eyes, then swings his legs over the side of the bed and sits up, gazing up at me through dark lashes. His eyes look more black than silver in this lighting, but they are mesmerizing all the same. "Come here."

I move toward him without conscious thought, stopping when I'm standing before him.

He lifts his hands to my hips, resting them there for a moment before pulling me onto his lap. I gasp, grabbing his arms to steady myself, and settle into his lap.

"What are you doing?" I ask in a quiet voice, my pulse kicking up at his hooded gaze.

"Nothing you don't want me to," he says, nuzzling my neck and making me shiver with anticipation. His lips drag along my skin, peppering kisses in their wake.

I lean into him, pressing my breasts into his chest as I tilt my head to give him better access to my neck. My pulse pounds beneath my skin, waiting for the sharp sting of his fangs in my neck, but it doesn't come. I shouldn't be disappointed by that, and yet...

"I can't stop thinking about fucking you," he says, his breath hot on my skin. "The way you felt wrapped around my cock... I'll never get tired of it."

"So fuck me," I offer, shivering at the thought of having him inside me again.

He chuckles deeply and leans back to meet my gaze. "You know, I figured you'd say that."

"So cocky," I murmur, running my fingers through the hair at the back of his neck and gripping it as I start grinding against him.

His grip on my hips tightens and his eyes narrow. "You're asking for me to flip you onto my bed and fuck you until you're screaming my name."

"Big talk," I taunt, bearing down and putting pressure on his groin, circling my hips against him.

He groans, tipping his head back. "Fuck, that feels good."

My core clenches with need, throbbing at his words. I keep going, the sight of him like this pushing me to move a little faster. "Mmm," I purr, closing my eyes as I continue to grind against him. He hardens against me, pressing into the heat between my legs. I lean down and touch my lips to his in a whisper of a kiss before moving my mouth to his ear. "I want you inside me."

With that, he makes good on his threat to flip me onto the bed. From one second to the next, my back is pressed into the mattress, and I'm staring up at him as he leans over me, his unruly dark brown hair falling into his eyes.

"Happy to oblige," he says with a devilish grin.

"You know, I figured you'd say that," I echo his words.

He seals his mouth over mine, kissing me slow and deep as I run my fingers up his chest, lifting his shirt to expose the tight muscle underneath.

"Will Gabriel be home soon?" I murmur against his lips.

He nips my bottom one. "Should be. You want him to join us?"

My heart races at that, because hell yes I do, but I don't want to stop and wait for him either. "Maybe next time." I kiss him again. "Have you heard anything from the others?" Another kiss. "Where are they?"

His mouth freezes against mine. "Calla," he says in a low voice, leaning back and bracing himself with his hips on either side of me, holding me down. His eyes search mine for a moment, and he tilts his head. "I would've thought you'd be a little more creative than this."

I frown, gripping the sheets on either side of me. "What do you mean?"

"Trying to seduce me for information." He tsks, shaking his head. "I'm disappointed."

"Seriously?" I laugh and reach for him, but he moves too fast, grabbing my wrists and pinning them above my head with one hand. "Kade—"

"Nope," he says, cutting me off, though he doesn't genuinely seem mad. "You're going to keep nice and quiet for me now." He lets go of my wrists just long enough to pull my shirt off before trapping them against the mountain of pillows at my head. His eyes drop to my breasts, and he uses his free hand to trail an agonizingly slow path from my collarbone to the lace of my bra. He licks his lips before unclasping the bra from the front. My breasts spill out, my nipples stiffening at the cool air. Kade makes quick work of palming one, and when he lowers his mouth to the other, my back arches off the bed. He pushes me back down, swirling his tongue around my nipple before sucking it hard.

I gasp sharply. "Kade."

He pulls back and glares at me with dark eyes. "Quiet," he reminds.

I pull my bottom lip into my mouth, chewing it to keep myself from speaking again, and nod.

He drops his mouth to my other breast, giving it the same attention, while his hand slides down my stomach, making my breath hitch when he reaches the waistband of my jeans. He pops the button easily, pulling the zipper down so slow, I have to grit my teeth from scowling at him. He's teasing me on purpose. There's not a damn thing I can do that won't result in him stopping what is making my body come alive, and we both know it.

Kade pulls his mouth off my breast and kisses down my stomach, making my skin tingle at his every touch. He nips my hipbone, making me lift off the bed. He lets go of my wrists, giving me a stern look that says, *keep them there*, and I obey. His fingers curl around the waistband of my jeans, and he pulls them down with my panties to just below my knees, baring my center to his hungry gaze.

My heart slams against my ribcage as he lowers his mouth to my navel, pressing a feather-light kiss there before moving lower, kissing the inside of each of my thighs before dragging his tongue along my slit. My cheeks fill with heat as I watch him between my legs, and I grip the pillows at my head when his lips close around my clit. He sucks gently, making my head spin. I close my eyes, lifting my hips to push his face closer, but he flattens his arm across my waist, holding me down as his tongue dives inside, devouring me completely.

I suck in a breath, and I can't stop the moan that escapes my lips. He plunges in and out of me with his tongue, bringing me new levels of pleasure. And when he uses his fingers to spread me wider for him, my eyes shut of their own accord, my chest rising and falling fast with shallow, labored breaths.

Kade brings me to the edge with his mouth. Licking and

sucking until I explode, clenching around him and squeezing his face between my thighs, desperate to hold him there.

As I come down from my earth-shattering orgasm, Kade tugs his shirt off, tossing it behind him before sliding off the bed and tugging his pants down. His cock springs free, and my eyes immediately go to it. *Fuck*. I'm not sure I'll ever get used to its size. I certainly won't get tired of it.

He crawls over me again, positioning himself at my entrance. He drags the head of his cock along my slit and presses hard against my clit, making me gasp. "You're ready for more already, aren't you?"

I open my mouth, then clamp it shut, nodding instead. I lean up and reach for him, pulling his mouth down to mine and kissing him hard, putting all of my desire into it so he knows just how ready I am, just how badly I want him.

His lips move against mine as he spears me with his cock, groaning against my lips. The muscles in my thighs clench at the invasion, but I wrap my legs around him and force him in deeper. He kisses me long and slow, pushing until he's inside me to the hilt. He holds still for a moment, giving me time to adjust to him before he starts moving in slow, small thrusts. His lips leave mine, kissing along my jaw until he reaches my neck. His tongue finds my pulse, and his lips close around it, sucking playfully.

My head spins, and I lift my hips to meet his thrusts as they get faster and deeper. I'm racing to the edge once more, and when Kade's mouth finds the sensitive spot between my shoulder and neck and he sinks his fangs into my skin, I cry out, clenching around his cock. His thrusts quickly become harsh and quick. His mouth seals over mine, and the taste of copper fills my senses. I kiss him back, clinging to him as he pounds into me. A few more thrusts and he stiffens, releasing inside me as my tight inner walls squeeze him.

I break the kiss as he pulls out of me, both of us breathing hard. Warmth leaks out of me, and Kade uses the sheet beneath us to clean me up. I swallow past the dryness in my throat, watching him in a haze of pleasure.

"Guess I'll be doing laundry today," he says with a smirk, falling onto his back beside me.

My lips curl into a sated grin as I stare at the ceiling. Sweat clings to my skin, and my heart is slowly coming down to a normal pace. I sigh contentedly, and Kade chuckles in response. I slide my hand along the silk sheet until it finds his, then entwine our fingers, giving him a quick squeeze before I pull away and force myself to get up. I slide my legs over the side of the bed and plant my feet on the hardwood, giving myself a second before standing. My muscles shake in protest, but I manage to stay upright. I collect my clothes and walk backward to the door, Kade's eyes on me.

"Where are you running off to?"

"The shower," I say, "and then, unfortunately, I need to study. Which is far less exciting than this was."

He props his hands behind his head. "You could just forget studying, and we could do that again."

I press my lips together, warmth spreading through me at the offer. It sounds a hell of a lot better than my assigned reading for this week, but there are more important things I need to do before Lex and Atlas get back—and not knowing when that will be definitely puts me at a disadvantage. "Maybe later? Could be a nice reward for getting through my homework."

"I feel so used," Kade says in a teasing tone.

I hold my clothes to my chest and shake my head at him. "I think you'll live," I say before turning and walking out of his bedroom, closing the door behind me. I let out a heavy breath and hurry to the bathroom connected to my room where I take the quickest shower of my life.

Once I've towel-dried my hair and gotten dressed, I leave my room and walk down the hall toward the stairs leading to the second floor. I hear Kade's voice coming from his room. It sounds as if he's on the phone, though his tone is calm, so I don't bother trying to overhear. I don't have any time to waste.

I hurry toward Atlas's office. Something tells me that if I'm going to find answers, this will be the place. He spends most of his time in here, always behind closed doors, so this has been—and probably will be—my only opportunity to snoop. My hand freezes halfway to the doorknob. I shake it out, shoving down my nerves the tinge of guilt I have for the invasion, and slowly open the door. I slip inside, closing it behind me as gently as I can. When it clicks into place, I whip around and cross the room in a few hurried strides, reminding myself that Atlas and the rest of the guys know virtually everything about my life, and not because I chose to share it with them. I'm not saying the whole tit for tat in this situation is right, but my ever-growing need to figure this whole thing out overpowers the weight of my guilt.

My stomach sinks when I realize Atlas took his laptop with him. I shouldn't be surprised, and honestly, the odds of me being able to guess his password to get into it would have been pretty much nil anyway.

I walk toward the wall of bookshelves and skim them. Most of the books are non-fiction, business-related tomes. There are a few shelves filled with some of the classics—first editions, no doubt—but nothing that will offer me any clarity on what's going on.

I try the filing cabinets on the other side of the room, but they're all locked. I grit my teeth, scowling at myself. As much as I want to believe I wasn't putting so much hope in this search revealing the guys' plans, I can't help the heavy blanket of disappointment draped over my shoulders.

Walking back to the desk, I thumb through a few stacks of loose paper. It's mostly bills and some junk mail. There's a copy of my class schedule, my signed apartment lease, and some credit card statements that go a couple of years back. A few weeks ago that would creep me the fuck out. But now? It's just a drop in the bucket.

Sighing heavily, I drop into Atlas's ridiculously comfy leather chair. I spin around and glance out the window at the trees along the property for a few minutes. When I turn back, I grab the edge of the desk, my gaze catching the letterhead at the top of a piece of paper sticking out from under a bill for pool maintenance.

*Ellis Industries.*

"What the...?"

Why does Atlas have something with Brighton's family's business on it?

I pull the paper free and scan it, my heart in my throat as I realize what it is. A stock register. But why... why would Atlas buy stocks in an environmental company? My head spins, and I shake it, trying to clear the jumbled thoughts all trying to come through at once.

Holy shit. Not only does he have stock in the company, he's a majority shareholder. He may as well own the damn thing.

The paper falls from my hand and floats onto the desk. I stare at it, trying to make sense of this, but I can't figure it out. I press my hands against the desk calendar and frown at its unevenness. I lift the calendar and find a file folder. Pulling it out, I flip it open and gasp, the air leaving my lungs in a vicious *whoosh*. I'm staring at a photo of Brighton and me at brunch, but my hair is significantly shorter. This picture was from last year.

My heart pounds as I flip to the next page. And the next. More photos of Brighton and me. Then some with just

Brighton. *Surveillance photos*, I realize after a handful of them, and my stomach roils. Her class and work schedules are next, along with call and text logs, email chains, and bank statements dating back before I even met her. But why would they be tracking Brighton before she was even part of my life? It doesn't make sense.

I press my fist against my mouth, my vision blurring with hot tears as my head spins with so many questions I can't think. Pushing the chair back, I stand on shaky legs, and the folder slips out of my hand, the papers spilling onto the floor. I don't bother picking them up. I'm already heading for the door.

## 18

I pace the length of my bedroom, gripping my phone in my hand so tight my knuckles are white. I rake my fingers through my hair, messing up the already frizzy waves.

I've texted Brighton five times in the last thirty seconds.

*Brighton, we need to talk.*

*I have to tell you some crazy things that won't make much sense, but I promise I'm telling the truth.*

*Please answer me. I'm freaking out over here.*

*Where are you? I'll come to you.*

*Brighton?!?!*

My heart lurches when the text bubbles appear in our conversation, and I chew my thumbnail as I wait for her reply.

*Jesus, Cal. What the fuck is going on? I'm at home.*

I let out a relieved breath.

*Stay there,* I type, *I'm on my way.*

Pocketing my phone, I stop in the kitchen and leave a quick note that will hopefully, if nothing else, buy some time.

*Studying on campus with friends. Please don't be creepy and show up uninvited. Be back later. xx, C*

My chin trembles as I drop the pen beside the notepad and walk toward the front door, slipping out and closing it quietly behind me. I couldn't hear Kade on the phone when I rushed back to my room after discovering the stalker folder Atlas had on Brighton, so I can only hope he's passed out in his bedroom.

I desperately want to pack a bag and hightail it out of town with Brighton, but I can't. That would lead the guys right to her, and I couldn't do that. I have no idea why they're interested in Brighton or her family, but my gut tells me I need to warn her. They haven't done anything yet that I know of, but that doesn't mean they aren't planning something.

I can't help but wonder what Brighton knows. She's never expressed interest in her family's company before—or in politics. How is the Ellis family connected to Atlas? Do they know one of their shareholders is a vampire? In my search for answers, I only ended up with more head-spinning questions.

My stomach twists into knots as I order an Uber and jog down the street to the main road to catch it. I can't risk waiting at the house for Sylvie—who has a 5-star driver rating and can't wait to help me to my destination, apparently—to pick me up there.

Once I'm in the back of the car heading toward Brighton's apartment, I finally take a deep breath, letting it out slowly in an attempt to calm my racing heart. I have no idea how Brighton will react to what I'm going to tell her, though if her response to me telling her about vampires almost a month ago is any indication, it's going to take a while to get through to her.

"How's the temperature back there, sweetie?" Sylvie asks, glancing at me through the rearview mirror.

"Fine, thanks," I say, staring out the window as my knee bounces.

"Oh, good! There's a bottle of water in the cup holder if you're thirsty."

I force a smile as my response, and when she opens her mouth again, I add, "Sorry, I'm just not really in the mood to chat."

She nods and says nothing for the rest of the drive. I feel bad, but I can't think about anything else right now. I'll be sure to tip her generously and leave a good rating when I get out.

When we pull up outside Brighton's building, I unbuckle my belt and thank her for the ride. I get out, shutting the door as I step onto the sidewalk. The cold air whips through my hair, chilling my cheeks and making me shiver and tug my jacket tighter.

Sylvie pulls away, speeding down the empty street, and I slide my phone out of my pocket to text Brighton so she can let me into her building.

I type, *I'm here*, but before I can hit send, I'm grabbed from behind, and my phone goes flying, smashing against the concrete. I don't have a chance to yell as I'm dragged from the sidewalk, down the space between Brighton's building at the one next to hers. I try to scream, but the hand clamped over my mouth muffles the sound, and the next thing I know, I'm being shoved into the back of a black SUV. My head smacks one of the tinted windows, making me cry out in pain as my vision blurs from the impact.

Finally, my vision rights itself, and I find myself staring into an unfamiliar silver gaze.

I blink hard, my heart slamming against my ribcage as dread coils in my stomach, and my voice cracks as I say, "Dante?"

"Sleep."

Awareness creeps in as I pry my eyes open, and the first thing I see is a massive fireplace with crackling flames. Soft jazz music fills the space along with the faint scent of lavender. I try to look around without moving or alerting my captor that I'm awake.

I quickly come to the conclusion that I've been brought to a fancy penthouse. I'm sprawled on a couch next to a coffee table where a large candle is burning, which is likely where the lavender scent is coming from. The windows on either side of the fireplace show a darkening sky outside and are draped in heavy gray curtains.

Holding my breath, I peek over the back of the couch and exhale when I don't see the vampire that grabbed me off the street.

My pulse spikes. *He found me.* And the guys won't know I'm in trouble because I lied about where I was going. Not that I want to be around any of them right now, but if the alternative is the psycho vampire that's been hunting me because of some ridiculous claim he believes to have over me, I'll take the evil I somewhat know over the one I don't at all.

Either way, things really aren't looking good for me.

I crawl off the couch, tiptoeing around the large, open room. Everything is neutral tones, mostly white with gray accents, and a little feminine. On the other side of the couch is a long dining table with chairs on one side and a bench on the other. There's an ornate mirror hung on the wall behind the table, making the space appear even bigger, and a crystal chandelier hung above it. I fight the urge to scoff at all of it. I've gotten used to fancy living quarters living with the guys, but this is next-level.

"I'm glad to see you're finally awake."

My stomach plummets, and I whirl around to find the vampire who grabbed me off the street. His black hair is slicked back, accentuating the sharp angles of his sun-kissed face. He's dressed as if he just came from a business meeting, in a navy collared button-up, black slacks, and shiny black dress shoes. He's staring at me with a glint of interest in his eyes that makes me want to vomit all over the marble floor at my feet.

He tilts his head, sensing my discomfort, and a slow smile curls his lips. "It's nice to finally meet you, Calla."

I swallow the lump in my throat. "I'm sure you can understand why the feeling isn't mutual," I force out. "Dante."

He chuckles deeply and steps toward me.

I reel back, bumping into the bench at the dining table. "W-what do you want from me?"

Dante sighs. "Must we discuss that right now? I'd would much rather enjoy some time together first. You've captured the attention of some very powerful vampires, Calla. Color me intrigued."

My eyes narrow. "Jealous much?"

"What is it about you that convinced them to let you live?" he muses aloud.

I clench my jaw to keep from saying something I might regret. Which is becoming more difficult every time this guy opens his mouth. "Why exactly do you want me dead?" I ask instead.

"An eye for an eye," he says. "It's nothing personal. You see, I got screwed over when those boys of yours intervened in my business all those years ago."

I blink at that, faintly wondering how old the vampire in front of me is. He appears older than the guys, which I imagine would be determined by the age he was when he was turned—if he was turned. In human years, he looks to be in his mid-thirties. Vampire years, though? I don't want to think about it. "Your *business* that could've cost my ancestor his life."

He shrugs. "We all make choices. He made the decision to go into business with certain people, and instead of facing the consequences of that, he got bailed out."

I cross my arms over my chest and straighten my posture in an attempt to trick myself into believing I'm not terrified of this guy. "He's dead," I say flatly. "Why should I have to face the consequences of something I wasn't even involved in?"

Dante purses his lips before they twist into a smirk. "You try that one with Atlas?" He shakes his head before allowing me an opportunity to respond. "How about Gabriel? He's always had a soft spot for beautiful humans."

My stomach twists painfully at his words. I don't want to think about Gabriel—or any of the guys—with another human.

Wait, what?

When did *that* happen?

Despite the confusion and fear surrounding what I found in Atlas's office, the thought of never seeing them again and finding out the truth makes my eyes burn. As much as I've tried to fight what I feel about being with them, they've taken care of me since arriving in my life like a hurricane. Whatever is going on with them and Brighton's family, I want to be around long enough to find out what it is.

"So what," I say, "you'll feel better about what you lost after killing me?"

He cocks his head to the side, staring at me. "Do you know what I lost?"

"Whatever it is, you're of the opinion that my life is worth less, so I really don't care."

"Hmm, you're a feisty one, aren't you?" His eyes glimmer with what I can only describe as hunger, and it makes me want to run far away. "Perhaps I should keep you around a while. I think you and I could be good friends, Calla."

"Are you offering me a choice between your company and immediate death? Because if you're going to kill me anyway, I think I'd prefer you do it now."

Amusement colors his features, and he laughs. "Kade must get a kick out of your fire."

I roll my eyes. "Your issue is with them. Why don't you take it up, you know, *with them?*"

The humor in his eyes morphs into something darker, something that triggers an alarm in my head. *I need to get out of here now or I'm not going to.*

"Oh, I intend to. When I deliver your cold, lifeless body to their doorstep."

Nausea rolls through me in a vicious wave, and I inch backward. "How theatrical of you." I force an uninterested tone despite Dante being able to hear the erratic heartbeat in my chest.

He appears right in front of me before I have the chance to register any movement. He wraps his fingers around my throat and tugs me forward, flashing his fangs as a sharp gasp escapes my lips. I've got nowhere to go. When he opens his mouth and his fangs extend, my breath gets caught in my throat.

"Please don't." My voice cracks, and I cringe inwardly. The thought of having his fangs in my neck brings tears to my eyes and makes bile rise in my throat.

His chest rises and falls deeply with an inaudible sigh. "I could make it so much better than what you've experienced. You have no idea, little human." He tips his head back slightly to look into my eyes. "There's no reason for your death to be painful."

I shake my head as much as I can in his grip. "Dante, please don't do this."

His fanged smirk makes my stomach feel as if it's filled with rocks as he leans in slowly. I'm frozen in place, stunned by fear and weighed down by the knowledge that there's no chance I can escape him. No one knows where I am; I don't even know how long I've been here. The only shot I have at making it out of this alive is if Brighton contacted one of the guys after I didn't show up. They could track me here—wherever *here* is.

Dante pulls me out of my thoughts, grabbing my hip with his free hand and digging his fingers into my skin. I yelp in surprise, and the sound quickly turns to that of pain when he sinks his teeth into my neck. I try weakly to push him away, shame and terror rippling through me as the pull of my blood leaving my body fills me with dread.

This is nothing like what I experienced with the guys. This is the worst thing I've ever felt.

"Please," I whimper, silent tears slipping free and wetting my cheeks even as I keep my eyes closed. The room no longer smells of lavender, but the strong, copper scent of my blood as it spills down my neck, staining the front of my shirt.

He doesn't stop; his teeth are like a hundred needles in my neck, ripping and devouring me in the most grotesque way I ever could have imagined. Worse, actually. This feeling, this horrific pain is nothing I could have anticipated or prepared for. My head spins, and I force my eyes open, only to find the world darkening around the edges of my vision. I open my mouth to scream, a final effort with the minuscule amount of strength I have left, but before the sound tears from my lips, Dante goes rigid against me. He makes a choking sound as he pulls away from my neck and stumbles to the side, reaching for his heart—or where it should be.

Instead there's a gaping hole in his chest and blood soaking through his dress shirt.

His mouth opens in a silent scream, his fangs covered in my blood, and then he collapses onto the floor, revealing the most stunning woman I have ever seen... who just so happens to be holding Dante's heart in a perfectly manicured hand.

I stumble back a step into the table bench, and it's the only thing that keeps me upright. My eyes go wide, and if my jaw wasn't locked, I would probably scream. I lift my hand to my neck, covering the puncture marks as they continue to drip blood down the front of my shirt. My chin wobbles, and I swallow hard, desperate to keep it together. The panic in my chest is making it hard to breathe, and I can't look away from the vacant-eyed vampire between us. *He's dead.* I should feel relieved, and a part of me definitely does, but I have to fight the dark ripple of sadness and remind myself that he was going to kill me. Dante was going to drain my blood even as I begged him to stop, then drop me on a doorstep all because of a deal that went sideways over a hundred years ago.

The woman tosses Dante's heart at his feet, and it lands with a sickeningly wet *thud*. "Such a waste," she says with a sigh, shaking her head. Her hair is so blond it's almost white and reaches past her breasts. Her silver eyes are shadowed with dark liner and she has lashes any woman would kill for. Her lips are dark red and pressed in a tight line as I stare at her.

"I... um, th-thank you," I whisper as the blood seeps through my fingers, leaving a trail of crimson along my pale skin, and I cringe.

The elegant woman bends—the white floor-length dress she's wearing pooling around her feet—and rips a length of Dante's shirt from his body, rising as she uses it to clean his blood from her hand. "Do not thank me, Calla." She drops the blood-soaked scrap of shirt onto the floor. "Dante's ill-mannered, silly little excuse for revenge is not the reason you were brought here."

Confusion floods through me as I grip the table behind me, quickly joined by intense dizziness from losing so much blood, and I frown at the woman who I believed was *saving* my life.

She smiles at me, the light from the chandelier above the table catching her fangs.

I choke on a scream as the woman shoots forward with vampiric speed, and her sharp silver gaze is the last thing I see before my world goes dark.

## END OF BOOK ONE

READ BOOK TWO NOW! mybook.to/temptedbyfire

If you enjoyed *Bound in Crimson*, please leave a review on Amazon and Goodreads. Reviews are so important for authors to find new readers!

Join J.A. Carter on Patreon at www.patreon.com/authorjacarter for exclusive access to signed paperbacks, bonus content, early cover reveals and book releases, plus so much more!

Sign up for the newsletter at www.authorjacarter.com/newsletter-sign-up.

Follow J.A. Carter on Instagram and TikTok (@authorjacarter) to stay up to date with all of the things!

Join J.A. Carter's Reader Lounge on Facebook for first looks and exclusives!

ACKNOWLEDGMENTS

Thank you to my amazing friends and family for all you do. Your support and encouragement keeps me going on days when the words don't come easily.

To my cover designer, Keylin Rivers, thank you times a million for all the back and forth and being so patient with me.

To my lovely beta readers: Ashley, Jennifer E., Lindsay Hamilton, Allie Foster, Sarah, Lindsay McCracken, Haileigh S, Kathryn Stilin, Amanda, Ellen Jorene, Heather, Charlotte Brown, A.L., Tessy Dockery, and Harriet James. No amount of thanks can express how grateful I am for your feedback and excitement for this book! You all rock, and I hope you enjoy the finished story!

Finally, thank YOU, incredible reader, for giving this book a shot. *Bound in Crimson* is my first reverse harem, and I've have a lot of fun exploring the different dynamics and relationships between the characters, more of which you'll get to see throughout the entire *Blood Oath* series, so stay tuned!

xx,
   J.A. Carter

Milton Keynes UK
Ingram Content Group UK Ltd.
UKHW012155141023
430633UK00005B/440